"Why are you ashamed of your body, Clare?"

Lazar's eyes roved over her scantily clad figure as she answered tautly, "I'm not."

"Oh, yes, you are," Lazar dismissed her answer. "I have seen you in nothing but dresses you could wrap around your slender shape three, maybe four times."

"I like loose-fitting clothes," she defended herself. "Anyway, it's nothing to do with you."

"Of course it is. That's why I bought you that swimsuit. I was sure that underneath all that material you'd be worth seeing. Your body is beautiful, such loveliness...."

Clare had heard enough. Anxious to cover the revealing swimsuit, she made a grab for her dress. Trepidation grew as she felt his arms come around her.

She had been afraid of men—with good reason—for a long, long time. And Lazar Vardakas was no ordinary man!

Devil
in Disguise

by

JESSICA STEELE

Harlequin Books

TORONTO · LONDON · LOS ANGELES · AMSTERDAM
SYDNEY · HAMBURG · PARIS · STOCKHOLM · ATHENS · TOKYO

Original hardcover edition published in 1980
by Mills & Boon Limited

ISBN 0-373-02424-X

Harlequin edition published August 1981

Printed in U.S.A.

CHAPTER ONE

CLARE heard the phone in the hall start to ring while she was upstairs making the beds. It wouldn't be for her, she knew, but she had better go and answer it in case Bruce, one of her two brothers, was outside and hadn't heard it.

She was at the top of the landing when the phone stopped ringing, and bending to pick up a duster dropped from her pocket, not meaning to eavesdrop, she heard Bruce say, 'Hey, that's a great idea!' his voice all excited. 'Ten days, you said? Of course I'll come.'

She smiled. She loved her parents, Kit and Bruce, very much, anything that made them happy made her happy. About to return to her bedmaking, she stopped dead on hearing the excitement go out of Bruce's voice.

'Oh, I've just remembered,' he said, 'I can't.' She waited and then heard him say, 'My parents are away on holiday and—er—I've promised Dad I'll have a job done for him when he comes back.'

What job? True, their parents were on holiday. After much 'Shall we—shan't we' they had gone off yesterday on a motoring holiday touring France. But Clare was sure there wasn't a thing Dad had asked Bruce to do in his absence.

'Thanks all the same, Rob,' she heard him say. 'I'll be glad if you'll think of me another time, though.'

She heard the ping as the phone went down and stood for a moment in silent contemplation. Rob Edmonds was a friend of her brother's, as keen a potholer as Bruce was. Had he been asking Bruce to go potholing with him? Bruce would love that. He was on holiday too, all three of the Harper men were. There was no earthly reason why he should not go, no reason at all—except her.

Her brow puckered as she thought, not for the first time, that the reason for her father closing the family architect offices down for two weeks was solely so that she would have one or other of her brothers near at hand if she needed them while her parents were away.

Feelings that had started to grow in her lately of being just slightly stifled by her family's over-protective attitude began to stir in her again, and with those stifled feelings came a mixture of guilt. Her family were the most wonderful in the world and, true enough, she had needed their support. But now, now she was for the most part over the shock of that dreadful day five years ago that had robbed her of her power of speech for a time, it just wasn't fair that they should go on making sacrifices for her.

Bruce was twenty-six now, Kit twenty-four, and though they both had friends and went out a good deal, should the event occur that meant her parents had to go out unexpectedly, as had happened when Grand-dad had been so ill before he died, then either one of her brothers would drop everything so Clare should not be left on her own at night. For the first time ever, her parents had gone on holiday without her. And now, by the sound of it, Bruce was giving up a chance of a holiday with Rob Edmonds so that he could take turns with Kit in being with her when dark descended.

The bedmaking forgotten, Clare left her position on the landing and went downstairs. She found Bruce in the kitchen, the kettle on the boil, and knew if she asked what his call had been about he would hedge and fob her off.

'I was just going to make some coffee,' Bruce said, seeing her there. 'Want some?'

'Please,' she said, gathering her courage to tackle her tall lean brother whom no amount of home cooking would fatten up.

She felt quite shaky inside at what she had to do, for she had never consciously made a decision in her life; her decisions had always been made for her. She sat at the kitchen table and waited while he filled two mugs and came to join her.

'Did Rob Edmonds ask you to go potholing with him?' she asked, barely before he had the chair beneath him, and while Bruce looked at her startled, his face giving away that that was what his phone call had been about, Clare went on—boldly for her. 'You know, Bruce, there isn't a thing you have to do for Dad. I heard him say to both you and Kit yesterday that you can forget the office for two weeks, that there's nothing there that can't wait until you all go back.'

'Hey, what is this?' Bruce exclaimed, slowly recovering from his surprise in seeing the first signs of aggression in his sister.

'Oh, Bruce,' sighed Clare, her aggression vanishing, 'I'm spoiling everything for you—for all of you, aren't I? It's because of me you won't go, isn't it?'

Straightaway he denied it, but she wasn't fooled. 'Don't be daft, Clare,' he said, his voice full of derision as he leaned forward to playfully tug a lock of her silver-fair hair. 'You're spoiling nothing. I made up that excuse about having to do something for Dad because

I couldn't think of anything else on the spur of the moment.'

Had she not heard the excitement in his voice at the start of that conversation, Clare realised she might have been fooled, and she had cause to wonder then how many other pleasures had had to be forgone because of her.

Sadly she shook her head. 'It won't wash, Bruce,' she said. 'You want to go, I know you do.' Then with a resolve about her that surprised her as much as her brother, 'When is he going? Today?'

'About twelve, he said,' Bruce told her before he had time to think.

'In that case you're going with him,' said Clare, feeling determined. And before he could protest, she looked at the kitchen clock. 'It's five past ten now, it won't take half an hour to get your gear together. You can go and ring Rob while I start packing for you.'

'Not so fast!' Bruce halted her as she got to her feet.

'Oh, Bruce, please go,' Clare pleaded, seeing he hadn't moved and didn't look to have any intention of moving. 'I'm better now, you know I am. And anyway, since Kit will be here you have no need to worry about me.'

'Yes, but Kit might want to go out,' Bruce pointed out, then sucked in his breath, aware he had inadvertently let out that they took good care to see she was never on her own in the evenings.

'If he does he can drop me off at Aunty Katy's on the way and pick me up on the way back,' she argued, realising that now wasn't the time to go into the subject of her always having someone with her when darkness fell. 'And anyway, he plans to spend his holiday taking his car to pieces. He's in town now getting some parts for it, so I doubt he'll be going far with his finger nails grimed with sump oil.'

With a determination about her that was alien to the girl she had been, it took Clare another fifteen minutes to badger her point of view home. But it wasn't until Bruce saw that it was something she really wanted, that it got through to him how dreadful she would feel if he didn't go, that he went to make the telephone call she was so insistent on.

At a quarter to twelve he had been ready for some time, but was staring out of the sitting-room window looking down the drive for some signs of their brother Kit.

'He's probably had trouble tracking down a control box in Guildford,' said Clare. 'Look, you're going to be late if you don't get a move on. Rob won't want to hang about if he's ready too.'

Bruce took his eyes from the window to look into her earnest brown eyes. 'I'd have liked a word with Kit first. I've no idea where in North Yorkshire we'll be staying or when I'll be able to get to a phone.'

'Bruce Harper,' said Clare, trying to look cross, 'we had all this to-do with Mum and Dad, insisting they forget about us and the village of Halesbridge for the two weeks they'll be away. You were as firm as Kit about their not phoning us.' She smiled, a thing she rarely did, unaware of how beautiful she became when her solemn features lit up. 'Don't let me have the same hassle with you!'

'You're getting assertive in your old age,' Bruce teased his nineteen-year-old sister. But after a bit more badgering he said if it would please her he would keep away from any telephone he happened to come across.

'Kit will probably turn up the minute you're gone,'

she told him, knowing he was still worrying about not seeing him. 'Please go, Bruce.'

She went out into the August sunshine to see him off, feeling quite a sense of achievement as she went back indoors. Kit would be back any time now, and she hoped he would feel as glad as her that Bruce had been persuaded to do something with his holiday.

There was always washing to do with three men around, so while she was waiting for Kit she set the machine going, glad to have the company of its noise in the quiet house as she pottered around doing various jobs. She had helped her mother in the house ever since she had left school. It was a fairly large house and though with the business doing so well they could easily have afforded to employ domestic help, Ruth Harper had declared she would rather do her own housework, and with Clare to help her they soon got through it.

There had been talk of her being trained for something, Clare mused as she went to empty the waste basket at the garbage can, but nothing had come of it. Though recently she had begun to think that the decision to keep her at home had been more because they were afraid for her if she went out into the outside world, and she thought again what a lot she had to thank them for.

And yet something she couldn't define was stirring in her. What it was she couldn't have said. Guilt that she was always their first thought? Guilt that each in turn felt responsible for her? Even her brothers, she thought, had this strong sense of responsibility for her. She didn't have to look further than the tussle she'd had with Bruce before he'd gone on his way.

Two o'clock! Kit was late. She went to the sitting room window to look down the drive, and was just in time to see Kit turning in, a cloud of exhaust smoke trailing behind his Spitfire sports car. He was in a hurry about something, she thought, pangs of alarm clutching at her. He usually had much more respect for his vehicle than to take the corner like that.

She hurried outside to meet him. He was lanky like Bruce, though where Bruce had a thatch of unruly dark ɪ ɪr, Kit was blond.

'Something wrong?' Clare asked urgently when he cut the engine.

'How would you . . .' he asked, pausing deliberately, she thought, 'like to spend two beautiful, glorious, chance of a lifetime weeks, in superb, magnificent— Athens?'

'Athens? Greece?' she exclaimed.

Kit's excitement overrode his pretence at being casual as, unable to hold back any longer, he enthusiastically told her that while waiting to be served with his car parts, Peter Nolan, a friend of his, had joined him in the queue and, looking as sick as a pig, had told him that he was on holiday too. That he and his fiancée Lynn had planned to fly to Athens early that same evening for a two-week holiday, only that morning Lynn had come out in spots that had been diagnosed by the doctor her mother had summoned as measles.

'Bearing in mind I'd waived my fee because of our friendship when I did the plans for the house he's having built, and so enabled him to afford this holiday, he offered me his flight tickets and said I could take over the flat he's rented for the fortnight. So,' he asked, his blue eyes alight at the idea, 'what do you think, Clare? Shall we go?'

Excitement fluttered in Clare too. She had read a

good many travel books, and Greece had tremendous appeal. She would love to see Athens.

'You've got your passport from that trip you took with Mum and Dad last year, haven't you?' Kit went on. 'And since I have mine, we haven't got any problems.'

She had forgotten until Kit had reminded her. Of course he had been all fired up to go to Greece last year, only he had gone down with 'flu the week before and hadn't been able to afford to go since because he had given himself a get-well present of the Spitfire that had cleaned him out.

Stepping over the door of the car, Kit draped a careless arm across her shoulders and walked with her into the house, talking excitedly of what they would do once they were in Athens, unaware that she hadn't yet said she would go.

'Where's Bruce?' he asked as they entered the kitchen, going on to say that if Bruce could get a flight out he could join them in Athens the next day or sooner if it could be arranged.

The thrill Clare had felt at the thought of actually seeing Athens for herself left her. Suddenly she was realising that in all fairness she couldn't go—not when she had already got Bruce to take a holiday on his own. It seemed only fair to her then that Kit should have the chance of having a holiday on his own too. Her mind became too busy in working out how this was going to be achieved for there to be room for her to wonder how she was going to feel at being left in the house on her own.

'Do you mind if I don't come with you?' she asked an astounded Kit. 'The thing is I—er—thought I'd like to have some new curtains up in the sitting room when

Mum and Dad return. Mum and I saw the material she liked when we were in Guildford one day last week.' They had too, so that part wasn't a lie.

'You mean you'd rather stay at home making curtains than come to Greece with me!' exclaimed Kit in astonishment.

'I promised myself I'd have this surprise ready for Mum,' Clare told him, knowing she'd have to try and make him believe it. Knowing too that he mustn't know Bruce had gone away because there was no way she was going to get him to leave her once he knew that, and not a chance in a million that he would take notice of her saying, as she had to Bruce, that she would feel awful about it if he didn't go on his own.

'You can make curtains any old time,' Kit pressed, not seeing anything wrong with the curtains presently adorning the windows.

'You go on your own—why don't you?' said Clare, her mind looking for ways to excuse Bruce's absence. 'You were ready to last year, and I'll be all right with Bruce if that's what's worrying you.'

He neither confirmed or denied that it did worry him, but asked again, 'Where is Bruce?'

'He went to see Angela Micklewright in Guildford— he's only just gone. Didn't you pass him?'

'Must have gone the other way,' said Kit absently.

'I don't think Bruce will want to go away,' said Clare, her mind busy, glad to remember that Angela didn't have a phone. 'He's been seeing a lot of Angela just lately.'

'Has he?' Kit asked as though he hadn't noticed. Clare hoped Bruce would forgive her lie. 'What time did he say he would be back?'

'About six, I think,' she answered, and seeing a

frown on Kit's face, risked, 'Definitely no later.'

'That'll be too late. I have to be at the airport by then.'

That he had said 'I' and not 'We' gave Clare hope that things were going her way. But as with Bruce she found she had quite a tussle on her hands before Kit finally agreed to go.

One of the shirts he wanted to take was part of the wet washing, but after Clare had overcome all his arguments against going, it was a small matter to find him another one that would do as well. 'You can always buy one in Athens if you run short,' she told him, and knew she had been right to make him go on his own when his eyes lit up at the word 'Athens'.

It wasn't too bad in the house after Kit had gone, but as dark descended and she drew the curtains and doubly checked the safety chains were on both outside doors, Clare began to have doubts about the wisdom of what she had done. The house was so quiet, every sound magnified. Telling herself she was lily-livered was no help at all, and made not a scrap of difference to the way she was feeling. She turned on the television, and found some comfort to have sound in the room for all she had no particular interest in the programme.

But it was when she went to bed that her real nerves beset her—so much so that she was in two minds whether or not to make up a bed for herself on the downstairs settee, as being upstairs gave her a feeling of even more total isolation. If only she had some sleeping tablets. But she had been off those for ages now. Oh, what if that dreadful nightmare returned! She hadn't given a thought to that when sending her brothers off.

She lay down, but left the light on, trying to remind

herself that that terrifying nightmare was an infrequent visitor these days. It must be all of six weeks now since she had woken up in the middle of the night to find the light on, her mother and father with her, Bruce and Kit hovering anxiously in the background, her screaming having got everyone out of bed.

She tried to read for a while, but the house creaking had her eyes going to the door in alarm time and time again. She always slept with her door open, but tonight, feeling the need for a different sort of security, she had closed it. Angry with herself for being such a poor-hearted creature, she tossed her book down and buried her head under the clothes, giving serious thought to getting into the Mini she shared with her mother tomorrow and going to ask her Aunty Katy if she could give her a bed until Bruce came back.

After a terrible night when every hour had her sneaking a look at the clock, Clare finally went into a deeper sleep as a comforting daylight crept into the room. At eight o'clock she got up, and once washed and dressed felt on top of the world that she had done it. She had actually gone through one night on her own! She felt so proud of herself, all thought of going to Aunty Katy's was forgotten.

But Sunday night, once darkness descended, followed the same pattern as the previous night, and she was overwhelmingly relieved to see dawn break.

When it came to bedtime on Monday night, if it hadn't been for the fact that she had left it too late to go to Aunty Katy's and that it was dark outside, she was sure she would have got out the Mini and raced round there hammering to be let in.

It had gone midnight when she heard the sound of a car in the drive and sat bolt upright in bed, her heart hammering painfully. She heard a car door slam, and for one petrified moment couldn't think where the phone was so she could ring for help. Even her legs felt paralysed with fear as her seized brain let up sufficiently for her to recall that the phone was down in the hall where it had always been. She couldn't go down those stairs—she couldn't!

Someone ringing the door bell had her nerves jumping with apprehension. Perhaps they would go away if she didn't answer it, she thought. Then the ringing came again. Oh God, they'd be able to see the light on in her room from the front of the house! The ringing stopped, only for the sound of what to her agitated state seemed like giant fists to start banging on the wood panelling.

Chewing at her bottom lip, she fought against the coward she owned herself to be. Then finding some inner strength, she reached for her summer dressing gown at the bottom of the bed.

Noiselessly she tiptoed down the stairs, her heart thudding in her ears, jumping again as she reached the hall and heard a fist crash once more against the oak front door.

'Who—who is it?' she asked as she reached the door, her voice sounding high and squeaky. She realised her pathetic attempt at speech could not possibly be heard. 'Who's there?' she asked more loudly, and in her highly strung state could make no sense of the answer she received.

Silence reigned on both sides of the door, then deep masculine tones were saying something about Kit—something about Kit and an accident.

Clare's fears for herself vanished in that instant. With shaking fingers, knowing it was the police outside, she groped for the light switch, flooded the hall with light, then switched on the porch light, and was about to take off the safety chain before caution that hadn't waned any over the last five years had her hands coming away to go to the door catch and pull the door open a few inches.

It wasn't a policeman who stood there—not a uniformed policeman, at any rate. This man didn't look like a policeman at all, the thought shot into her head as her anxiety for Kit became mixed up with anxieties for her own safety. The man standing there had black hair, a tanned skin from what she could make out, and he was over six feet tall.

'I am sorry to disturb you,' he said in faultless English, though with her emotions all confused Clare wasn't sure that there wasn't a trace of a foreign accent there somewhere. Her apprehension quickened and she was sure he could tell she was nervous when he gave her a reassuring smile before his face sobered and he added apologetically, 'But it is important that I see Mr Edward Harper.'

That smile should have reassured her, but she had learned not to trust. Though she did begin with an automatic, 'He's ...' before she broke off. She had almost said he wasn't in, and she mustn't do that. This man looked charming, didn't look as though he would harm her, but ...

'What about?' she questioned, and when the man made no move to ask to be allowed in, the remembrance came that she had only opened the door because she thought he had said something about Kit, and she had only one anxiety then. 'My brother,' she said quickly. 'Did you say Kit ...'

'You must be Clare,' the man said, just that suggestion of a foreign accent coming through. 'I am sorry to have to tell you, there has been an accident.'

'Accident—Kit?' Her brain went numb.

'I received a call at my London hotel about an hour ago from my brother in Greece,' the stranger went on, breaking the news to her gently. 'I thought since the accident happened on my property that I should come and acquaint your family with the news personally.'

Clare felt the colour drain from her face. It hardly registered that this man must be Greek and a property owner, as her mind filled with dread about her brother.

'He's—he's—Kit's not—*dead*?' she asked in a hushed voice.

'No, no,' she was quickly assured. 'His condition is grave, but not critical.' He paused to give her an encouraging look. 'Perhaps if I could come in and speak with your father ...' he suggested.

Her worries all for Kit, Clare's natural caution disappeared. Yes, yes, he must come in. She had to know all there was, had to know if she could help in any way.

'Just a moment,' she said quietly, quickly closing the door to release the safety chain, forgetting entirely she was dressed only in her summer robe, uncaring of how she looked with her cloud of silver-white hair tousled about her shoulders. Even her shyness with strangers had gone when she re-opened the door and stood back to allow the man over the threshold.

Five feet six and slender into the bargain, she felt dwarfed by the man who stood by her side. He too was lean, though with a breadth of shoulder that spoke of powerful muscles. For one frightened moment she thought of nothing as she witnessed his eyes, as black as night, on her hair as though he couldn't believe the

colour was real, then he had collected himself and remembered the sombre reason for his visit. It seemed
to her then that though this was her home, the command of the man took charge from that moment on.

'Shall I wait while you call your father?' he asked,
politely not moving from where he stood just inside the
hall.

Running distracted fingers through her hair, un-
intentionally drawing the stranger's eyes to it once
more, Clare stammered an invitation for him to follow
her into the sitting room, and her legs went weak sud
denly so that she just had to sit down, glad the stranger
had decided to sit too, because it was too much for her
then to have any sort of conversation having to look
up so far.

'My name is Lazar Vardakas,' he told her when she
hadn't complied with his request to call her father, and
it was as though he, the stranger, was out to put her at
ease. 'If you will tell your father . . .'

'My father is away on holiday,' she found herself
telling him. 'My mother too.'

'Oh,' said Lazar Vardakas, looking surprised and
thoughtful. Then, as though trying to recall what else
he had been told over the phone, 'But you have another brother, I believe,' he searched his memory some
more, 'Bruce, isn't it? Perhaps I might see your brother
Bruce?'

That he seemed to think that only the male members
of her family could deal with this particular crisis
touched on her only lightly as she thought fleetingly
how charming Greek men must be that their women-
folk must be so guarded. But what impinged on her
more was that considering they were a family so un-
known to him, Lazar Vardakas seemed to know a

tremendous amount about the Harpers. Of course—he had mentioned having a brother too. Perhaps Kit had got friendly with his brother before his accident; he must have told him something about them. But now wasn't the time to worry about that. He had said Kit's condition was grave, but not critical, and she had to know more. Almost absently, she told him:

'Bruce is away on holiday too.' That seemed to surprise him far more than the surprise he had shown that her parents were away, but she had other things on her mind, so it hardly bothered her. 'You said Kit's condition is grave . . . ?'

'You are in this house by yourself?' he questioned, his very tone comforting, so that had she thought she would have found herself sitting in her thin wrap entertaining a stranger as short a while as half an hour ago she would have known herself terrified at the very idea, instead she found herself confirming without alarm:

'Yes, I am. Kit didn't know Bruce was away. I'm afraid I didn't tell him.' Oddly, at that moment, she blushed, and didn't know why other than she felt guilty that this stranger should know she wasn't above deceiving her family. Yet she could never explain, she hardly knew why herself except that this urge to know a little independence had been trying to get through for quite some time. Yet oh, how she wished they were all back with her now!

Lazar Vardakas seemed not to notice her blush, and as gently as he could he told her, 'I would have preferred to have spoken with the men of the household. Indeed, I was hoping . . .' He broke off as though he knew what he had been hoping would not now come to fruition, and began to tell her how Kit's accident had come about.

'I own a small island called Niakos where my brother Aeneas was having a few days' break from business. Whether Aeneas met your brother in Athens or whether your brother made his own way to Niakos, I am not sure. But Aeneas must have taken a liking to him, because we do not encourage casual visitors to the island. However, your brother admired in particular one of the horses kept at Niakos and Aeneas, believing him to be an accomplished horseman, allowed him a ride.' His face was solemn when he added, 'I regret that your brother took a very bad fall.'

'Oh,' said Clare, chewing at her bottom lip. Kit did ride occasionally, but his main interest was his car. Oh, poor Kit! He wasn't usually headstrong, but perhaps he had thought it would be letting the side down to jib at riding some brute of a horse he just wasn't up to controlling. 'You said his condition is grave,' she reminded him. 'What exactly ...'

'He has severe concussion. A doctor was summoned from Athens immediately, of course,' she was told, 'and his prognosis is that he should recover well. The only trouble is ...' he seemed to hesitate as though not to worry her further.

'The only trouble is—what?' she asked hurriedly, her fears for Kit growing.

Reluctant to add to her distress, Lazar Vardakas studied the carpet beneath his feet and said slowly, 'Well, to tell you everything, your brother Kit seems to be off his head with worry about you, his sister.'

Clare could have cried with anguish then. She could just imagine Kit, who like the rest of them was forever watching out for her, writhing in a tortured delirium for her safety, somehow knowing he was powerless to come to her aid and save her from whatever gremlins were in his head.

'He has spoken of all his family during this semi-sleep he is in, but his anxieties for you in particular are keeping his head from resting,' she was told regretfully.

'Oh, poor Kit!' was wrenched from her, and she just didn't know how she kept back the tears. She felt so helpless, so powerless to do anything. She knew Lazar Vardakas wasn't deliberately telling her the worst, and thought with the concern he was showing that it was more probable he was keeping far more from her than he was telling.

'Naturally, as the accident happened on my property, on one of my animals, I feel that I am responsible,' he went on. 'As soon as I leave here I shall fly to Greece to see if there is anything I can do.'

Ridiculously, with so much else buzzing around in her head, Clare found herself asking, 'Can you get a flight at this time of night?'

'I have my private plane standing by waiting for me,' he said matter-of-factly, and almost to himself added, 'I had been hoping I might be able to take your father or perhaps your other brother back with me, but ...' A thought seemed suddenly to have occurred to him. 'You have your parents' forwarding address?'

Clare shook her head. An idea was beginning to stir, and she wondered if she had enough courage to act upon it. 'My parents are touring France. I have no idea where ...'

'Your other brother—Bruce. You have his holiday address?'

'No,' she said, feeling guilty again. 'I know it must sound awful to you,' she added, remembering reading somewhere that Greeks had a great feeling for family and trying to defend her own, 'but my family don't know I'm here on my own. I—er—tricked Bruce and Kit.'

He stood up, and she knew he didn't think much of what she had just told him. But she couldn't let him go, not yet. She had to find the courage from somewhere to act on her idea, to speak up and ask him if he would take her with him. After all, she reminded herself, she had sat here alone with him, scantily dressed too, she thought, catching sight of her robe, and no harm had come to her. He reached the sitting-room door, and the thought of Kit writhing in torment gave her small courage a boost.

'Mr Vark—Vadarkas,' she said, getting his name all mixed up. He halted, a politely enquiring look on his face. 'Er—would you like a cup of coffee?'

'Thank you, no.' He had the door open.

'Can I come with you?'

It came bursting out in a rush. She saw his eyebrows ascend for all the world as though he thought she was suggesting something improper, but she gabbled on while she had the courage.

'If Kit is as ill as you say then I just know he won't get well again until he sees me. Please, oh, please take me with you!'

For long painful moments he looked at her, then to her relief his hand left the doorknob. His look was stern when he said:

'Your brother says you are nineteen. Is that true?'

Clare wasn't sure what that had to do with it, though perhaps if she could convince him she was of age he might agree to take her with him.

'Yes,' she said, trying to keep calm and feeling on the brink of the biggest adventure of her life—if he agreed.

'You look no more than fifteen,' he said coolly. 'You have a passport?'

Did he mean so that he could check her age or so that she could go with him?

'Yes, yes. Shall I go and get it?'

For a long while he studied her pale face, recording her clear brow and huge brown eyes, his look taking in her sweet nose and generous, now tremulous mouth.

'You will need to bring it with you,' he said succinctly.

CHAPTER TWO

EVERYTHING happened so fast afterwards that Clare found herself seated with Lazar Vardakas on his executive jet before she had time to wonder again if she was doing the right thing. She couldn't possibly doubt it from the point of view of getting Kit well again. And really it was more than rewarding to know she wasn't quite the faintheart she had always regarded herself.

It hadn't taken her long to throw a few things into a case. All her clothes were of the loose-fitting variety and would be just the thing in which to nurse Kit back to health. Would they allow her to nurse him, though? She had never before had anything to do with wealthy people, but a private plane, a private island, must mean that the Vardakas family had money. Well, she and Kit couldn't afford the services of a nurse, so she would have to tell Lazar Vardakas that, and then perhaps he would allow her to look after Kit.

She looked across at him, his head deep in some paperwork as they flew into the night. He must be a very busy man, she thought, weariness about her now the hustle and bustle of getting ready in the minimum amount of time was behind her. It must be two o'clock in the morning by now; she didn't want to draw attention to herself by taking another look at her watch, but he was working away as though night or day work had to be done before he allowed himself to close his eyes.

Clearly he was a man who did not forget the slightest detail. She had come down the stairs, her suitcase in her hand, to find he had come out into the hall. He had taken her case from her and when she would have led the way to the front door, he had stopped her, saying, 'Perhaps you should write a note for the milkman.'

At that point, understandably with all that had happened, she thought, her brain had seized up and even the simplest note to the milkman was beyond her. With a suggestion of a smile upon his face, Lazar Vardakas had handed her his pen and ripped a piece from the telephone note pad, instructing her to write, 'No milk until further notice.'

The throb of the plane seemed quieter now, or perhaps she had just got used to it. Lazar Vardakas sat opposite her, a table to the side of them on which his briefcase rested. His head was bent over his work, giving her an opportunity to study him. Her study confirmed what she already knew: Lazar Vardakas was very good-looking. The thought bothered her, but mainly, she realised, because she was so unused to seeing men as anything other than just 'men'. His eyes were as black as night, she recalled, unable to see them now as his lids shuttered them, but he had a very fine nose, straight and arrogant—though he hadn't been arrogant with her. Stern perhaps, but for the most part courteous, charming. He had been a little stern perhaps when she had dared her courage and asked if she could come with him. In all, he had done everything he could to ease the pain of what he had to tell her. Her eyes fell to his mouth. It was a warm mouth, she decided, that bottom lip showing a sensuality in his nature that had been absent in his dealings with her.

Ashamed that she could look at any man and think about his sensuality and not a little disgusted to find herself having such thoughts when before tonight just the very word would have her curling up within herself, she gave herself up to wondering about his age. All this was a deliberate effort to keep her thoughts from Kit and the wild speculation of wondering if he would be improved by the time they got to him—or would he be deteriorating rapidly?

Lazar Vardakas would be somewhere in his middle thirties, she decided, though she was unable to see any grey in his hair. Without knowing it her eyes fell to his legs, seeing the hard muscle of his thighs beneath the material of his lightweight suiting. As soon as she became aware of where her eyes were fixed, she hurriedly raised them, and went a fiery red as she looked straight into the eyes of the man who had given her permission to fly with him, all too well aware that he knew she had been making a study of his thighs.

His look was tight, as though he hadn't liked what she was doing, as though he didn't like her very much for that matter either.

'Mr Vad ...' Oh dear, she'd got it wrong again, though she had no idea what she wanted to say—to apologise perhaps. And then he gave her a slow smile.

'You appear to have difficulty with my name. Perhaps

you should call me Lazar,' he invited.

'Thank you—Lazar,' she complied, wishing she was more worldly, for he was being so nice to her and she must seem to him to be unsophisticated in the extreme.

There was still that quiet smile about him when he asked, his manners perfectly charming, 'And may I be permitted to call you Clare?'

'Please do,' she said eagerly, only just stopping herself from gushing all over him that he seemed ready to forget she had been giving him a close inspection.

'You will excuse me getting on with my work, I hope,' he said, 'but I shall be taking a few days off ...' He left the rest unsaid, and she felt guilty again, this time because, with his high sense of family, he was going to leave his work to take her to the island where her brother lay ill.

'Why don't you try and get some sleep?' he suggested, and for the first time teasing. 'I promise I shall wake you when we land.'

Unused to smiling freely, Clare's lips were tormented apart, and she wondered if she'd done something wrong, if she wasn't supposed to smile when teased, for his brow came down in a frown as he looked at her. Then the frown disappeared, and he said coolly:

'Or perhaps you would care for some refreshment?'

He's fed up with me, she thought, as she saw his eyes flick to his paper work. She resolved there and then that he wouldn't even know she was aboard until the time came for him to tell her they had touched down at the airport in Athens.

'I think I'll sleep for a while,' she told him with quiet dignity, and closed her eyes.

It was perhaps an hour, two hours later, that a

feeling of something threatening her had Clare's eyes
coming open. They stayed open, a dreadful fear shoot-
ing through her. For Lazar Vardakas was bending over
her, his face close, nothing about this hard-eyed, dark,
unsmiling man to remind her of the charming man who
had escorted her on board. This man wore the look
of the—devil!

She shrank away as far back as her seat would allow,
her eyes haunted, terror-filled, her heart set up a hammering of panic. Too late she realised she had been
wrong to trust him. This man meant her harm!

The exclamation, 'No!' ripped from her hoarse
throat.

Lazar Vardakas looked mildly surprised at the note
of fear that reached him, then he smiled and became
again the kind, charming man who had called at her
home to tell her about Kit. And she knew it must have
been a trick of the light that had made him seem so
terrifying. She felt ashamed to be such a panicky
creature, especially when he said in comforting tones:

'I promised to wake you—we are about to land.'

Clare sat sick with embarrassment wondering what
he thought of her mind, while, unperturbed, he fast-
ened her seat belt before returning to his seat to do
up his own.

He seemed to be well known at the airport and saw
her through passport control with the minimum of fuss,
a firm hand beneath her elbow as he escorted her outside to wait while he unlocked the door of a Mercedes
convertible.

A puzzled frown creased her brow. Somehow she had
expected Athens airport to be bigger than this. But she
had been placed in the passenger seat, their luggage

stowed before she found her voice to comment on it, and by then he had the car in motion and was pulling away.

'The airport was smaller than I imagined it would be,' she said shyly, trying to get over the feeling of having made a fool of herself just before they landed, and wondering as she spoke if he was the type of driver who preferred his passengers to stay quiet. He didn't answer straight away and she felt her conscious effort to overcome her feelings rebuffed, deciding she wouldn't speak again unless he said something.

And then he said, 'I expect you are feeling a little disorientated,' going on easily as he directed the car into open country, 'One minute you were tucked up in the land of dreams and very shortly afterwards you find you are landing in a country new to you. You haven't been to Greece before?' he thought to ask.

'No,' she confessed, and wanted to say she had always wanted to visit his country, only she didn't in case he thought she was gushing. Then thinking her reply had been too brief, needed something tacked on, she saw dawn was about to break and that they had soon got away from residential buildings, and said, 'I expected Athens to be more built up than this.'

A pause followed her innocent statement, and for no reason she could think of she felt a finger of fear reach out and stab at her. Determined not to give in to it— look what an idiot she had made of herself before!— she turned slightly in her seat to look at him. Alarm grabbed at her again to see his face was a mask of coldness. And then that finger of fear became a hand, a hand that gripped and had fear taking a tight hold. For his good-looking face looked darkly hostile and as threatening as it had on the plane, and all she wanted to do then was to get out of the car, to get out and run away from him.

He must have become aware she was looking at him, for the mask of coldness vanished. He turned his head to smile gently, and she was comforted again, the realisation coming that he couldn't have slept at all since there had still been some involved-looking figure work on that side table in the plane prior to him putting it in his briefcase when she had woken up. Of course his face was stern when he wasn't looking at her; he needed to keep his tiredness at bay, to concentrate on his driving.

He was looking to the road ahead when casually he said, 'We didn't land at Hellinikon—Athens.'

'Oh,' she said in surprise, but reassured by his casual tone as much as the fact he was now being the charming Lazar Vardakas who had personally called at her home to speak to her father.

'We landed at Micra airport, Thessaloniki,' he enlightened her. 'Salonika,' he made the small translation from Greek.

Clare was silent for a moment, trying to place Salonika from her readings of Greece. 'We're in the north, then?'

'That's right,' he said briefly, not commenting that she knew that much about his country for all she had never been there.

The island he owned must be more easily accessible from Salonika, she thought, than from Athens. That was before she thought she must be as disorientated as he had said, because Kit had made his way to the island from Athens. Though Lazar had said he didn't know if Kit had made his own way there or if he had gone with his brother, so perhaps Kit had fancied himself as a yachtsman and had hired a boat for a whole day to ex-plored further and further into the waters of the north.

She thought about it some more, then finally gave up worrying at it. She had complete trust in Lazar Vardakas; not many men would have been so family-minded as to do what he had done. She just knew she could trust him to get her to Kit by the quickest route possible. Though that did prompt a question, since they had been driving for what must be an hour, the sun the most delightful orange ball in the sky, that for all she caught glimpses of the sea, so they must be driving along a coast road, Lazar had made no move to turn into any sort of harbour where he might have a boat.

'Do we have to hire a boat to get to your island, Lazar?' She tacked his name on the end because she wanted him to see how good her feelings were towards him, and he had asked her to use it, after all.

'I have a boat of my own at the villa,' he said with a brief glance in her direction before his eyes went once more to the road ahead.

She felt awful badgering him with questions, but had to ask, 'Are we going to your villa, then?'

'Yes,' he said.

'I see.'

What did she see? They were going to his villa. He had a boat there that would take them to the island of Niakos. Well, that was all right, though since he must be tired and the boat journey could take several more hours, she felt guilty about exhausting him further, for all he looked to be superbly fit.

'You'll rest awhile before we carry on—to your island, I mean?'

'I think so, if you can bear to wait. I will ring Aeneas
as soon as we get to the villa to find out how your
brother is.'

'Thank you,' she said politely, thinking how kind he
was to think of telephoning, knowing how anxious she
must be.

'I have had a room prepared for you at the villa,'
Lazar went on. 'I think you too should have a few
hours' sleep before we continue our journey.'

Clare remained silent, her admiration for the man
at her side growing. Were all Greeks as thoughtful as
him? He must have telephoned his villa, or got Aeneas
to do it for him, as soon as he had heard the news.
Possibly there were rooms prepared and waiting at the
villa just in case he returned with both her father and
Bruce.

Admitting to feeling weary herself, she wondered if
he would like her to talk to him to keep him awake
the way her father did when he had been at the wheel
for a long time. But search round in her mind though
she did for something to say, she was so unused to making conversation with strangers, she couldn't find anything, so she stayed quiet until the thought came to
wonder what work he did. Hoping he wouldn't think it
an intrusion, she asked:

'You work very hard, don't you?' then, stammering
because that sounded a bit blunt, 'I—I mean, you were
working in the plane.' She wished she hadn't got started
and felt herself go pink. He had already told her he
had been working then because with the accident to
Kit he was taking a few days off. Her family would
never be out of his debt. She tried again, forcing herself to go on. 'M-might I enquire what sort of work you
do?'

For a moment she had a dreadful feeling she had overstepped the mark of politeness, for all she thought it was a fairly average question.

'Shipping,' he said, then, 'We have arrived.'

And as Clare looked out he spun the wheel and drove some way down a hilly sweeping drive. The drive had a variety of trees either side of it, some she recognised as olive trees. There were bright red bushes and shrubs interspersed every now and then, and when trees and shrubs ended, she had a view of beautiful green lawns before Lazar swung the car round in front of a villa which was not at all as she had imagined. It covered only one floor, but it was *vast*!

Lazar helped her out of the car, greeting a Greek male servant who came hurrying out to them. Lazar exchanged some words in Greek with him, then took her indoors where he introduced Phoebe who was the male servant's, Rasmus's, wife.

'You wish for something to eat and drink?' Lazar enquired, ready, she saw, to give instruction to Phoebe for anything she wanted.

But Clare had got round to thinking she had put him to enough trouble, though she was anxious for him to make his call to see how Kit was.

'No, nothing, thank you,' she said, smiling shyly to Phoebe, who was dressed all in black.

Lazar said something to dismiss Phoebe, his eyes noting Rasmus go by with her suitcase, then he took hold of her arm. 'I will take you to your room,' he said, and with a smile that warmed her, for she was feeling ready to wilt suddenly. 'Might I suggest you will rest better if you get into bed?'

It was a good suggestion, and she smiled gratefully at him for making it. On their way they passed Rasmus

coming back again, then Lazar was opening a door
and guiding her inside a spacious, well appointed room.

'I hope you will be comfortable here,' he said formally, to which she answered she was certain she would
be. Though she wanted badly to remind him about
the telephone call he had promised to make.

'I will leave you now to telephone Niakos,' he said,
just as though he could read her mind, and she was
alone.

Not wanting to undress, thinking that at any moment
Lazar would come back to tell her how Kit was, Clare
wandered about the room, liking its good quality furni-
ture, its full-length window that slid back also acting as
a door. The view was gorgeous, giving a panoramic
vista of a beach and behind it the wide expanse of the
Aegean Sea. She gazed her fill for some minutes, then
turning back into the room she noticed that besides
the door she had come in by, there were two other
doors in the room.

Her curiosity aroused, she opened first the one door
and saw it was a luxuriously fitted bathroom, complete
with shower unit and a deep sunken bath of sea green.
Closing the door, she crossed the room, and with a
tentative hand opened the other door.

It was another bedroom—a bedroom that communi-
cated with her own! There was a lock on the door, but
no key, she saw after a hurried inspection. Her heartbeats started up a familiar frightened hammering as
her eyes took in that the room housed a double bed,
and that the bed had been made up. Who slept there?
Agitatedly she knew she would never get into the bed
that had been made ready for her until she discovered
who.

A sound by the outer door had her spinning round.

Lazar stood there, nothing on his face but the sort of respect she thought he would have for any guest. Her heartbeats steadied. As her panic went, so rational thought came, and she smiled one of her rare smiles. Of course—Lazar had been prepared for both her father and Bruce. It was just his natural thoughtfulness to put father and son close together. She closed the communicating door, hoping Lazar didn't think she had been prying, then she forgot about the other room as she realised he had come to tell her the result of his telephone call.

'Is Kit ... How is he?'

'Much better,' said Lazar, meeting her half way across the carpet, and allowing her a small smile. 'You have nothing to worry about. Your brother regained consciousness about an hour ago and asked for a bacon and egg breakfast.'

Totally reassured, for Kit loved his food above all else, Clare sent Lazar a beaming smile that lit her whole face and made her truly beautiful. 'Oh, thank you!' she cried, and felt so choked suddenly she was afraid she might make a fool of herself and begin to cry.

The expression on Lazar's face stopped her. For he was staring at her as though transfixed, his eyes going to her mouth with an expression that looked to her as if he was anticipating what it would be like to have the feel of her mouth against his.

Alarm bells jangled violently in her head so that she thought she was going to faint. She clutched at the end of the bed, backing away from him, his face swinging in front of her. His voice coming from a long way off, but sounding so natural, brought her round again.

'You are more tired than you know, I think,' he said evenly. 'In fact you seem to be ready to collapse from tiredness. Would you like me to summon Phoebe to help you into bed?'

Clare looked at him and could hardly believe tiredness had so warped her imagination that she had thought she had seen that look on his face. For his face now bore the ghost of a comforting smile, nothing of ill intent there at all, and again she was embarrassed by her imagination.

'No. No, thank you. I can manage quite well on my own,' she said.

'If you are sure,' he said courteously, and then left her.

Extracting her nightdress from her case, Clare allowed herself a wry smile. The best thing she could do would be to get into that delicious-looking bed and sleep some of her imagination away. It was daylight now, and she was safe in Lazar's villa. Her smile turned into a grin. What a muttonhead she was! She was as safe with Lazar as if she was back in the arms of her family. With that comforting thought in her mind, she climbed into bed, and not long afterwards she was sound asleep.

It was midday when she awoke and she felt better for her five hours' sleep. Then she remembered she should have put her watch ahead by two hours, only it had slipped her mind. Quickly she moved the hand round on her watch, then hurried out of bed to wash and dress in one of the loose-fitting Victorian print type dresses she had brought with her.

She had no idea how long it would take them to get to the island, though she suspected, since she couldn't recall there being too many islands in Northern Greece, that it might take some hours for them to get to the island of Niakos. Lazar wouldn't be very pleased to be kept hanging around because she was such a lie-a-bed, she thought, hurrying from her room and wishing he had sent Phoebe to awaken her.

She met Phoebe in the hall, who seeing she looked lost, smiled shyly and by sign language directed her to a room off the hall which Clare found to be a dining room.

As she had thought, Lazar was not very pleased she had slept so long. She saw him immediately she went into the dining room. He was sitting at a table, his empty coffee cup telling her he had just finished his meal, and his expression when he saw her, she thought, was downright forbidding.

Taking her courage in both hands, she approached him, rushing into abject apology. 'I'm so sorry—so sorry to have kept you waiting all this time. I had no idea I would sleep so,' the word, 'long,' tailed off into a whisper as she saw his eyes were cynically going over her. Her earnest expression, the fresh and innocent look of her, were lost on him as he appraised her sourly.

Oh dear, she thought, he's furious because I've kept him waiting. After having to drop everything to run round after her family, he was livid that she hadn't had the courtesy to take no more than just a catnap. But she couldn't help it. She hadn't known she had been so tired. Though since her two previous nights hadn't been all that restful, her sleep was bound to have needed catching up on some time.

Without getting to his feet Lazar unhooked a chair from beneath the table, an unspoken invitation for her to sit down as he continued to give her the same unsmiling look. She took the chair and sat primly, her hands fidgeting in her lap.

'I'm so dreadfully sorry,' she began again, and bit her lip nervously that he didn't look ready to accept her apology. 'You've been so kind,' she forced herself to go on, 'and have gone to an enormous amount of trouble, when really you could just as well not have bothered with me.' Inwardly she sighed, knowing she had badly offended his Greek code of common courtesy. 'Perhaps,' she suggested timidly, 'when you've finished your lunch——' She could see he already had, but was trying desperately to be tactful and not offend him further. But Kit had to be her first priority, she sorely wanted to see him. 'Perhaps when you're ready you could take me to see my brother? He must be ...'

She didn't get to finish. Savagely Lazar Vardakas interrupted her. 'What charming manners you have,' he sneered, no resemblance in this snarling, dark-haired man opposite her to the wonderfully kind man she had last night asked to take her with him. 'Charming manners,' he repeated, his savage expression not lifting, 'for the sister of a seducer of virgins!'

Clare just sat and stared at him. For several seconds her mind refused to believe what she had just heard. Then her eyes grew wide, incredulous, as the shock of what he had said penetrated; her face drained of colour, and she gripped the table in front of her hard.

'Wh-what are—y-you saying? Wh-what do you mean?' she gasped. Had he gone off his head? Did he have two personalities, one he used at night-time, o. e he used in the day?

'So innocent,' he scorned. 'Your seducer brother said you were. But he didn't know how you had tricked him and his brother so you could have your home to yourself in order to enjoy the freedom the not so innocent can enjoy when there is no one there to see what they are getting up to.'

What was he talking about? Desperately she tried to gather together her scattered wits, vaguely recalling she had told him she had tricked her brothers into going away and leaving her on her own.

'But—but that was only so they could have a holiday without me. They ...' She hesitated, not wanting to tell him too much, but finding she suddenly needed to defend herself. 'They look after me too much as it is,' she added.

'Then it is a pity for you that neither of your brothers is in a position to look after you now, isn't it?' he snapped, his face cold now after the snarling countenance that had been about him before, but his look no less frightening.

Fear clutched at her, making her want to get to her feet and run. But her legs felt like jelly—she knew she wouldn't make it as far as the door.

'I ... You ...' she choked, having difficulty in finding words as the knowledge came that something was terribly wrong!

Lazar Vardakas surveyed her ashen face indifferently, letting his eyes drift over the concealing print of her dress before bringing them back to her face. His expression took on a speculative look.

'You appear innocent,' he summed up. 'It could even be that you are.' A long deliberate pause followed that had her every nerve end screaming in alarm, and she almost went under as he added slowly, 'We shall see.'

'Wh-what do you mean?' came hoarsely from her dry throat. Oh God, where was her courage? More than ever she needed to find some spark of it now. She had to try and look brave even if she was almost dropping from the shock of finding that the man she had thought so wonderful such a short time ago was now showing he was a devil in disguise.

He didn't answer, but seemed prepared to sit there all day letting his eyes bore through her. And it was at that moment that a small flicker of courage came to her aid. With it came the realisation too that her spark of courage would go again very quickly if she allowed him to carry on a conversation that looked to be growing more and more personal about her.

'What did you mean—about Kit being...' She couldn't finish.

'A seducer of virgins?' He had no qualms about finishing it for her, and she half wished she hadn't asked him when that savage look came to his face again. 'Unlike your country, in Greece the virtue of an unmarried woman is sacrosanct,' he told her, his expression grim. 'A Greek man,' he said proudly, 'does not have to hope his bride will come to him untouched. He has every confidence she will be.'

'But...' she began to interrupt him, and was silenced by the lift of his hand.

'Thanks to your brother, my sister's chances of making a suitable marriage have been taken away from her.'

'Oh!' she gasped. Kit was a normal man, she supposed, having never so much as thought of such things before. But would he have done what Lazar Vardakas was suggesting? He definitely wouldn't unless the girl had been willing, she knew that for a fact. So it made nonsense of what he was telling her about Greek girls and their prized virtue.

Her courage rose again. 'Kit would never have touched your sister without encouragement,' she said with conviction. She flinched back, her courage sent flying when Lazar looked so violently angry at the suggestion that he leaned forward and she thought he was going to strike her.

'How dare you!' he thundered, then seemed to gain some control. Though control he might have, his voice was still thundering as he told her, 'Your brother took Sophronia to his flat where he plied her with drink so that she didn't know what she was doing. And there he seduced her.'

'He wouldn't,' she denied, no thought of courage now as a fierce instinct had her defending Kit. 'He's not like that. He's good. He's kind and gentle. I'll grant he m-may have had a—a—fling or two, but,' her voice grew stronger, her conviction evident, 'but never would he treat a girl in the way you suggest he treated your sister.'

Clare doubted the strength of her denial had got through to him, but he looked less angry when she had finished, though none the less dangerous.

'Your brother defends your virtue with equal intensity,' he said softly, his eyes once more going over her in a way that made her shrivel up inside. 'Sophronia, when she had recovered sufficiently from her hysteria on realising she had given herself to a man outside wedlock, told my father that he had spoken of his sister Clare at quite some length.'

'He did?' she asked warily.

'Oh, he said nothing you need be ashamed of, I assure you,' he said, mistaking her wary look. 'He had nothing but good to say of you— how sweet and gentle you were. In fact the whole impression Sophronia had of you was that you were protected by your family with as much fierceness as any Greek girl could expect from her people. When Aeneas told me everything that had happened, repeated to me everything Sophronia had said of you, I instructed him to go and question your brother on the subject of this "Clare" and to telephone me again.'

'This was before Kit had his accident?' Clare asked, puzzled that if they thought Kit was as black as this Sophronia had painted him, why then had Aeneas offered him hospitality on the island?

'Your brother has not had an accident,' Lazar Vardakas stated slowly. But as Clare's heart lifted, he added cruelly, '*Yet*.'

'You mean . . .' She couldn't believe what he was saying, that . . . But he left her no time for comprehension, going on to let her know that he was completely in charge of the situation.

'To return to what I was saying. Aeneas rang me again, telling me your brother was of the opinion that your virtue was as pure as the colour of your hair. It was then that I thought it might be an idea to come and pay you a visit.'

'You didn't come to—to take my father to see Kit?' She wished he hadn't become personal again by mentioning the white colouring of her hair.

'I knew your parents were away,' he said coolly, shocking her into silence for a moment while her numbed brain tried to register what he was saying.

'You—you didn't know Bruce wouldn't be there,' she choked.

'That was a stroke of luck. But provided you didn't have a face and shape that said it was unlikely you were marriageable material anyway, I was prepared to bring both you and your brother with me.' With a superior shrug, he added, 'It would have been no trouble to have shipped him out to Niakos to wait with your other brother.'

'Wait?' she echoed, thinking she would either faint from the horror of what was happening or go to pieces completely at any moment. 'What ...' the word came out thin and reedy, but the question had to be asked. 'What,' she said again, 'have they to wait for?'

'Why,' he said, savouring the moment, his black eyes pinning her huge brown ones so that she couldn't look away, 'so that I can avenge Sophronia uninterrupted.'

'Avenge?' she gasped, her brain refusing to take her any further.

'To see that you,' he began slowly, watching the way her eyes grew enormous, 'you, who have been guarded by your family in the same way my sister has been guarded, shall suffer the same fate that she has suffered.'

Unable to speak, robbed of words, Clare just sat open-mouthed and stared, all her senses so numbed she couldn't move a muscle. Then some part of her brain that hadn't frozen over recalled he had said something about marriage, though what it was escaped her.

'Are you ...' she asked, in a voice she didn't recognise but which must be hers since it was coming from her throat, 'are you asking me to marry you?'

For answer, he tipped back his head and a roar of disparaging laughter burst from him, the shock of which was like a slap across the face to her and brought her out of her shocked state quicker than anything else could have done.

'You can take any idea that I might want to marry you out of your head,' he told her, his tone as derisory as his laughter had been. And then—shockingly,

'Though I do intend to have you in my bed ...'

That was as far as he got. Clare wasn't waiting to hear any more. Regardless that her legs didn't feel as though they would support her, she had sprung to her feet and was racing for the door, no thought in her head of where she was running to, her only idea that of escape.

He caught her with firm hands just as she reached the door, and all coherent thought left her at the feel of those strong immovable hands on her. Like a wild animal she lashed out at him, her mind too violated by what he had said for her to care where she struck him.

But her blows glanced off him, were ineffectual as that firm grip proceeded to shake her into reason. She came to herself to find she was being held at arm's length, and felt relief on discovering he was making no move to touch her anywhere else. Her breathing ragged, she quietened, capable of only standing and staring at him.

He said something in Greek, a swear word, she thought, then sourly, 'What the hell did you think I was going to do to you?'

A sickness invaded her as the one hushed word left her. 'Rape,' she breathed, and saw his face take on a tight look.

Without ceremony he marched her back to the chair she had so rapidly vacated and pushed her hard down into it, making sure she didn't look to have the strength to race away again before resuming his own seat.

'I said,' he reminded her tautly, 'that you should suffer the same fate as Sophronia. My sister was not raped.'

Not believing she was actually in Greece, was actu- ally having this conversation when less than twenty-four hours ago she had been safe in her own little world, nothing more important on her mind then than the curtain material she intended buying today, Clare heard the stranger within her doing the talking.

'You're saying you mean to—to seduce me?'

'That had been my intention,' he said, and her heart lifted fractionally to hear the past tense, only for it to plummet to the ground when he added, 'I still intend to take your virtue.' He didn't look as though the prospect pleased him very much. 'But after that little display just now, I am prepared to let you come to me in your own time.'

'My own time?' she repeated, in no way understanding, if he didn't intend to seduce her, how he was going to set about taking her virtue. 'How . . .'

'I will not raise a hand to get you into my bed,' he told her coolly. And then she almost crumpled into a heap as he went on, 'But unless you come to my bed voluntarily, unless you make all the overtures by . . .' he shrugged as though the matter hardly concerned him, 'say, the end of the week, then the accident I spoke of your brother having will, make no mistake, be a certainty. Only then it will not be just concussion he will be suffering from. I will personally ensure that never again will he want to come to Greece.'

Her breath caught as it was sucked in at the horror of what he was saying. She gave a choking cough as, her eyes wild, she fought to overcome her panic.

'Kit's all right? Y—you haven't . . .'

'Aeneas assures me he is very healthy—at the moment. He is a prisoner on Niakos where he will stay until I make the telephone call that will release him.'

And, Clare thought, that would only be when she had done what this hard, unpitying man demanded of her. 'You're saying,' she managed to get out, knowing she had to continue, had to calm down and ask the question that was half frightening her to death so she should know she hadn't misheard him, for all his English was faultless, 'that in order to save Kit from— from probably being maimed for life,' she swallowed, 'I have to come to your b-bedroom and ... and ...' she couldn't think the words he had used, let alone say them, 'and get into bed with you?'

'You know which bedroom is mine, I believe,' he said sardonically, making her want to hit out at his superior face. 'I saw you taking a look at it just before you went to bed.'

Oh God! she groaned inwardly. And she had been unsuspectingly thinking how marvellously kind of him to think of putting her father and Bruce in adjoining rooms. But she mustn't think of the way he had been last night. That hadn't been the true Lazar Vardakas. This man in front of her was the real one, this devil of a man. She had to have something else very clear before she left him. Only as she opened her mouth, he seemed to read her thoughts.

'You have my word that I shall not be opening that communicating door to get into bed with you,' he told her, giving her a considering look. 'Though I should advise you—if you don't want your brother to end up feeling very sorry he so much as breathed the same air as a Vardakas—not to delay too long before you take the initiative.'

She saw pride in every part of him then, realised in that moment that once the honour of the Vardakas family had been tarnished, then it was God help the

family of the poor unsuspecting person who had tarnished it.

'Mr Var—Vardakas,' she said, glad she had at last
got it right, knowing it was no longer permissible to call
him by his first name, but hoping somehow she would
be able to get through to him. She had to make him
see that Kit wouldn't have done what he had said, had
to try and make him forget this idea he had for revenge.
'I ... Won't ...' It was no good, she admitted herself
terrified at the fate that might befall her, and her courage spent, she just wasn't up to stringing one single
sentence together.

He rose from his chair, a tall, towering man. 'What is
it you are trying to say, Miss Harper?' he queried.
'That you want to get it over with now, perhaps? That
you would like to come with me now; to undress me
so you can use me as your brother used my sister?'

Ever afterwards, Clare found a tinge of self-respect to
realise she wasn't totally the cringing, pathetic creature
she had begun to think of herself as being. Temper that
was a stranger to her soared into life for three glorious
seconds.

'You can go to hell!' she screamed at him, and
knocked her chair flying as she hurled herself from it
and towards the door, and out of his sight.

CHAPTER THREE

HER temper was shortlived. She was a shivering mass of
fear by the time she had gained her room, and she
jumped in trepidation a few minutes later when, after
a light tap on her door, it opened.

But it was not the vengeful Lazar Vardakas who stood there, but Phoebe, with a gentle smile, carrying a tray of food. Just the sight of food made Clare want to vomit, but it took her many minutes of sign language, which might have amused her had she not been so upset, to get through to the concerned-looking Phoebe that she didn't want anything to eat. Reluctantly Pheobe took the tray away, though as if she didn't fully understand she left Clare with a pot of coffee, a cup and saucer.

In agony with her thoughts, Clare ignored the coffee, her mind in a whirl, taking some minutes before she could isolate one terrifying thought from any other. As she tried a few deep breaths, fighting for calm and endeavouring to ignore the instinct that would have her tearing out of the villa, to run and keep on running, it came to her with mind-blowing dread that she couldn't run away. How could she? Kit's safety was in jeopardy. Lazar Vardakas had meant what he had said about an accident happening to him. Supposing she did get away, supposing she was lucky enough to make it to the main road, get someone to give her a lift to the nearest police station—always supposing she could make herself understood—the Vardakas family must be well known hereabouts. Wealthy and powerful, she suspected, and if all Greeks felt the same as Lazar Vardakas about the honour of an unmarried sister, then could she expect any sympathy? They would have to do their job, she saw that, but wouldn't they first contact Lazar to see what he had to say?

A quivering groan left her and she collapsed on to the edge of the bed. Once he knew she had contacted the police, would he, before the police could get to Niakos, have telephoned his brother Aeneas and instructed him to hurt Kit before the police arrived?

She put a hand to her mouth to check a dry sob. Kit whom she loved, Kit who had always been so good and gentle with her, was in terrible danger, a danger far more terrible than the dreadful danger she was in. She felt ill that his reprieve depended on her going through that door. She looked across at the communicating door through which she was supposed to go and offer herself, and felt so nauseated, the door itself seemed to loom so large and ominous that she just had to go outside where she could no longer see it.

Her feet took her away from the villa, away from the main road. What point in going in that direction? She just couldn't trust herself in her wild fear not to beg a lift should she see a passing motorist. She owed it to Kit to try and be brave, to try and find a way out of this horrifying predicament that would save him from physical violence and a way that would save her from having to go through that door and into Lazar's bedroom.

Entirely unaware where her feet were taking her, her mind too full with worry, she saw with surprise that she had reached the private beach belonging to the villa. Turning her eyes seaward, she gazed at the waters of the Aegean, looking at the sea that went on for miles and miles as though hoping she might find some source of inspiration out there.

A sound behind her had her swinging quickly about, the fine beige-coloured sand having muffled the tread of her persecutor. He was less than five yards away and she backed hurriedly when he advanced further. But his strides were longer than her stumbling paces, and a soundless scream left her when his hard hand came down on her arm to halt her in her retreat.

Panic with her, she pulled violently out of his grasp, backing some more as she cried, 'Leave me alone! I don't want—you!'

He made no move to come after her, but regarded her frightened look cynically as though he thought it was purely an act she was putting on to get him to change his mind about what he intended should happen between them.

'It was not my intention to come looking for you with seduction in mind,' he told her curtly, reminding her cruelly, 'I thought I had made it plain enough that the amorous approach should come from you.'

Clare felt her whole body break out into a sweat at that, and knew then by the determined look of him that he meant every word he said.

'I merely came to find out why you are not eating. You haven't had a thing inside your stomach since last night. Phoebe tells me you didn't want any lunch.'

If he thought he might get her to come to him quicker by pretending a concern for her she knew was entirely phoney, then he could jolly well think again! she decided, glad to feel anger spurt inside her where before she had felt too defeated to fight back.

'I don't want anything from you,' she said ungraciously. 'I'd rather go hungry than eat at your table.'

His chin jutted furiously, and it wouldn't have surprised her then if he had yanked her back to the villa and stood over her while she ate. Indeed, for a moment his look became so grim she thought he was going to do exactly that. She took a step away in fear of having that hard hand touching her again, and his jaw clenched as he witnessed her movement. Then suddenly he looked completely and utterly fed up with her.

'Then go hungry,' he bit out at her, and turned to go, striding in the direction of the villa.

For ten minutes more Clare stood exactly where she was, taking some small pleasure in the thought that she had for the first time in her life had to stand up to someone, and had actually won.

Her pleasure was shortlived as she gazed about her wondering what she should do now, having no intention of following the way he had gone. It still gratified her that after years of being a nothing kind of person, since knowing Lazar Vardakas she had discovered she had a temper, could be angry, albeit at the moment it only came in short bursts, she did have a small supply of courage. Though she didn't thank him that she was learning that she wasn't entirely the wishy-washy creature she had been beginning to suspect she was.

Gradually as she stood there, she became aware of the scenery, and as the breathtaking beauty of the spot where Lazar Vardakas had his villa began to fill her senses, so for a very short while did she become lost in the wonder of what nature had created.

To the right of her lay the sea, warm-looking, inviting to even a non-swimmer like herself. In front of her a sun-kissed beach that was broken some way away by a jetty, and behind the jetty a boathouse. She looked to the left where the land rose higher and higher, to hills covered with lush pine trees, the foreground grass green and inviting to a goat she suddenly noticed tethered to a tree, contentedly nibbling away. She turned to look at the villa and noticed now, where before agitation had kept her blind, that it lay in a semi-circle of forest with the Aegean at its front. A place of complete seclusion for any busy executive who needed somewhere to come and relax.

Her senses still filled with delight at her surroundings, she ousted Lazar Vardakas from her thoughts. To let him intrude would ruin such beauty, would have her feeling ill again. Her feet took her towards the pine trees, no conscious thought in her mind now of where she was going, only some inner being telling her that for a short while at least she wanted to be part of the peace and tranquillity of that scene. Some part of her hoped that once there in among those trees she might find rest from those thoughts that would have her running scared.

How far she walked, the sunlight breaking through the tall pines, or how long it took before she found a clearing and sat down in the still beauty of the wooded slope, Clare had no idea. But she was in no hurry to go back. Though the tranquillity of thought she had hoped to find was missing as again and again the knowledge refused to be kept at bay of what was to happen to her if she was to secure Kit's safe keeping.

At last it was the frightening cogitations she thought would drive her out of her mind that had her leaving the sanctuary of the pine woods. Unable to sit quietly, she stood up and retraced her steps back to the villa.

Having found a footpath, she turned to go left at an olive tree, and was almost up to the sliding glass door of her room when she saw Lazar standing there, and pulled up short. By the none too pleasant look on his face she guessed he was waiting for her. He saw her, but didn't move, and she knew she would have to go towards him if she was to gain her room. She went slowly forward, admitting she was more than a little wary of him.

He barely waited before she was level with him before he was biting, 'Where the hell have you been?'

'Where would I go?' she asked in return, her voice bitter. He knew as well as she did that Kit's physical wellbeing depended on her staying put.

His expression didn't lighten any as he grunted, 'I see you are aware that the phone call will be made asking Aeneas to act in my stead should you try to escape me.' Then, terminating the conversation, 'We shall dine in an hour's time. Make sure you are there.'

Clare stepped round him and into her room, telling herself she was going to ignore the pangs of hunger that had begun up on the hillside and were now gnawing away at her. She was glad of the coffee Phoebe had left, cold though it was, as thirstily she drank it down. Then, feeling hot, sticky and miserable, she found fresh underwear and a clean dress and went to the bathroom, placing a sturdy-looking linen bin against the door without too much hope that it would stop Lazar from coming in if the thought crossed his mind so to do.

Bathed, and dressed once more in one of her loose print dresses, she had to own that she was starving. She told herself she was only going to the dining room because she was hungry and not at all because she was terrified Lazar Vardakas might come to her room and escort her there by force.

He was already in the dining room when she went in, wearing black trousers and a fine rollneck black sweater, and to her distracted senses, he looked more menacing than ever as he looked her over.

'Do you not possess anything but bell tents in your wardrobe?' he enquired, nastily she thought, realising that because this was the only type of dress she ever bought he wasn't likely to see her in anything else.

'I must apologise for not wearing a dinner gown,' she

said, to her amazement discovering another first—she
had a touch of sarcasm in her make up too, or was it
just that she was fighting with everything in her not
to collapse in a bundle of frightened nerves? 'I hadn't
realised,' she went bravely on, 'that I'd come here
to ...' Her voice petered out as it quickly came back
why she *was* here. But she tried to get back on top. 'I
... I only packed dresses suitable, as I thought, for
nursing a sick brother.'

He ignored her reminding him that he had told her
countless lies to get her to come with him, and remarked, 'Then you didn't think to bring a swimsuit
with you either?'

'No,' she answered shortly, and could have told him
she didn't possess one, but she didn't, any more than
she could have told him that even if she had brought
one with her, nothing would have got her changing
into it. It was her opinion, if only she could have her
way, that he was seeing as much of her as he was going
to see of her right now. Anything else was unthinkable.

Lazar offered her a pre-dinner drink, which she refused with a short, 'No, thank you,' only wanting to
eat her dinner and go back to her room. She fully
intended not to get into conversation with him. If he
required an answer to anything he had to say, then she
was going to limit her answers to a brief 'yes' or 'no'.

But to her surprise, quite how she was never afterwards sure, maybe because at first he began by telling
her something of his own family, his parents and sister
living in Athens, Aeneas with his wife and family living
near by, that she found herself stringing complete sent-
ences together.

And by the time he had brought the conversation

round to her family, she had forgotten she had resolved to give him monosyllabic answers only. That
was, until the conversation got round to her personally, and by then her reasons for not wanting to talk
to him were that she knew anything she could tell him
about herself added up to what must be a very dull
person when set against the sort of women she was sure
he usually dined with.

'And what type of work do you do?' he enquired, as
the very satisfying meal came to an end and he passed
over the sugar bowl so she could spoon some into her
coffee, taking it for granted that she, like most of her
contemporaries in England, did a job of some sort.

'I—er—don't,' she said. Then in self-defence, 'My
mother prefers to do her own housework, so I help her
at home.'

'So,' his eyes were watching her too intently for her
peace of mind, 'you do not mix with other young
people of your own age during the daytime?'

'No,' she answered briefly, and wished she could have
added something to that—but there was nothing.

'How about the night-time?'

'What do you mean, the night-time?' she returned,
unlikely to tell him that she seldom went out after
dark, and certainly never by herself.

'You have boy-friends, of course,' he stated. 'With
your unusual colouring,' he added, his dark eyes on
her silvery-white hair, 'apart from the rest of your
beauty, there must be many eager young men coming
to your home to call.'

To tell him she had never had a boy-friend wouldn't
be believed, she saw, and a flush of pink stole across
her creamy skin that he thought she had beauty. Was
she beautiful? she wondered, doubting it as the wary

thought came that this might be a lead up to something she would far rather not know about.

'I don't go out all that often,' she said, hoping her answer would kill the conversation dead and taking a quick gulp of her coffee, anxious suddenly to be away from him.

'Oh,' he said, giving her that considering look again, and causing her to wonder what the 'Oh' meant. That was until he said, 'Do you have one special boy-friend who comes to your home——' he paused, then tacked on, 'You have a close—relationship with one man in particular?'

The very idea appalled her. 'No!' she said sharply, and was rash enough to add snappishly, 'There's no special boy-friend. If I want to go out at night I go out with my brothers or my parents.'

Immediately she saw the way one eyebrow went up she knew she had said too much. But it was too late to take it back, so she put all her faith in hoping he didn't believe her.

He didn't believe her. That much was obvious when his face took on a mask of coldness. 'Credit me with at least some intelligence,' he told her gratingly. 'I lived in England for a time when I was studying. I am quite well aware of how the code of behaviour for young women there differs from my own country. You have no need to try and make me believe you have never had a boy-friend. No need at all to lie to me.'

So she had told him she had never had a boy-friend, for all it had been in a roundabout way, and as she had suspected he didn't believe her. Well, she wasn't bothered what he believed, all she wanted to do now was to get to her room and away from the coldness in his face. She stood up, the remainder of her coffee unwanted.

'Why shouldn't I lie to you?' she found herself saying. 'You haven't cared about the lies you told me in order to get me here.'

He didn't answer, but fixed her with a sour-tempered stare she found unnerving. It had her leaving the subject of the lies he had told her, and she was asking:

'And anyway, what about you? Do you have a special girl-friend?' And as the thought struck, 'Are you married?'

'No, I'm not married,' he answered, his eyes taking on a devilish look that tormented her even before the sense of what he said next came. 'How could I be? Adultery is a legally punishable offence in Greece.'

As if that would bother him! And then it hit her, hit her what he was really saying, and as suddenly her senses were alarmed again. He was saying that because he was unmarried he would not be breaking that particular law by ... There was a hard aggressive look to him that had the thought screaming in that he didn't appear to be content to wait until she was ready to go to his room.

'Lazar,' she said quickly, in her urgency forgetting she had intended never to call him by his first name again, but stammering on because she needed his answer without delay. 'Y-you won't—I mean ...' Her hands were sweating as she tried to get the words out. 'It is still up to me to—to open that c-communicating door, isn't it?'

She waited, nausea welling up in her that he was taking his time in answering. From the look of him he seemed to think her question unworthy of an answer.

But she had to know, she just had to. And so she tried again.

'Please,' she said, 'p-please tell me you won't b-be—that you won't . . .' Her voice tailed off as his impatience with her got the better of him.

'For God's sake go to bed!' he snapped, standing up and towering over her, frightening her further, 'and drop this display of the terrified innocent!' But Clare found she couldn't move, not until she had the answer she wanted.

His eyes went deliberately from her wide pleading eyes to become fascinated by her trembling mouth. Then as he took his glance from her more full lower lip with its partnering perfect upper lip, his night black eyes looked into hers, and very quietly, he said:

'The prerogative in opening that door is all yours, my dear,' and there was something so sensuous emanating from the very air around him that her breath was stifled as he added, 'I shall be waiting any time you choose to call.'

Clare slept only fitfully that night, only half believing she could trust his word. But as dawn filtered through the night sky, she dropped into a lower depth of sleep, and awoke to a glorious morning that called her out of bed and had her going to take a shower.

Half an hour later she wandered from her room to be met by a smiling Phoebe who greeted her shyly with, '*Kaliméra, thespinis,*' and received Clare's own shy response of 'Good morning, Phoebe,' then directed her to the terrace where she saw a table had been set.

Fortunately Lazar was not anywhere about, and Clare was glad to breakfast alone, having been able to get through to Phoebe that all she wanted was fruit juice, toast and coffee.

Somehow, she thought, somehow today, now that the shock of Lazar's proposition had receded, she had to try and get through to him that what he suggested just wasn't possible. Yesterday she had been so sickened and alarmed by what he had said she had been able to do nothing to get him to change his mind.

She found the idea of tackling him scary, but it had to be done. He had given her until the end of the week to come to terms with his ultimatum. But he might just as well have given her a year, because she knew she just couldn't do it.

Having decided she wanted to have her interview with him as soon as possible, when Phoebe came to bring her coffee, with the aid of sign language, she was able to ask her where he was.

Panic, this time for Kit, had her in its grip when she learned he had gone out. She was terrified he hadn't waited until the weekend but had, after her display of fear last night, for all she had thought he hadn't believed in it, taken the boat she was sure must have been in the boathouse she had seen yesterday. She was certain he had gone to Niakos to deal with Kit personally.

However, some frantic signs to Phoebe assured her some few minutes later that he had gone out in his car and not the boat.

Yet when five minutes later she saw the Mercedes appearing round the olive trees that flanked the drive, the top open with a shirt-sleeved Lazar at the wheel, she was out of her chair and heading for her room, which had not been her intention at all.

Perhaps it would be as well to rehearse what she had to say to him, she thought, pacing up and down, knowing she had to get the courage from somewhere, had somehow to try and get through to him.

But she was to find she had no time for rehearsal. Because he could not have stopped longer than to halt the car in front of the terrace, for without him bothering to knock her door was opened and Lazar stood there. He hadn't waited to drop off his shopping either, she thought, seeing he was holding a paper bag in his hands.

She didn't want him in her room, and darts of panic had her speaking without thought.

'You can't do this,' she said on a gulp of fear that his visit meant he wasn't waiting for her to cross the threshold of his room.

'Do what?' he asked innocently, his eyes noting that she was wearing another of her 'bell tent' dresses.

'Y-you know,' said Clare, seeing he had left the door open and didn't look as though he meant to close it. Oh, if only her agitation hadn't got the better of her! If only she had waited for him to mention the purpose of his visit, she thought, the feeling growing since he was making no move towards her that he was still waiting for her to make the first approach.

Casually, he propped himself against the wall by the door, not saying anything, just waiting for her to continue. Damn him! she thought, glad of a flare of anger.

'Look, Mr—Lazar——' why pretend, she thought of him as Lazar more often than not, 'you must see that all this is wrong.' His face was inscrutable now, nothing showing to give her encouragement to carry on. Yet she knew she just had to, just had to try and get through to him. 'I c-can't do what you're asking,' she said pleadingly. 'I just can't—p-please don't make me.'

For one glorious moment she thought she saw a softening in him. Those dark eyes didn't appear to be as hard as she had seen them. But as he still had nothing to say, she pressed on with what she thought was her advantage, hope surging that he wasn't the devil she had thought him yesterday.

'Kit couldn't have done what you say he did. I know he couldn't,' she said, and saw straight away that she had made a terrible mistake in bringing her brother's name into it. For she had reminded him, if he needed any reminding, exactly why she was being made to pay in the way he had chosen.

'You are calling Sophronia a liar,' he said tightly, all the proud honour of his Greek forebears in every line of him as he pulled away from the wall and looked darkly at her.

She didn't dare say 'yes'; his very look intimidated her. 'Well,' she began, swallowing hard, 'I know my brother ...'

'Not as well as you thought you knew him, obviously,' he rapped. 'There is no doubt in my mind that Sophronia is telling the truth. She may be headstrong at times, even wilful when she cannot get her own way, but no Greek girl with her upbringing would invent such a story and so besmirch her honour.'

'But ...' Clare knew she still had to try. She couldn't leave it like this, not after having had the courage to bring the subject up. But Lazar seemed to think she had said quite sufficient.

'Enough!' he stopped her, his hand going up imperiously. 'I have told you what you must do. We shall not discuss it again. You have until Saturday to either accept that or let your brother pay for irrevocably damaging the whole of my sister's future.'

Her colour gone, she could only stare at this dominating man. And yet, as frightened as she was, something within her had to be heard.

'Lazar, *please*,' she begged, only to retreat a step as he took a step towards her.

But her panic for the immediate moment was not needed, for he came only as far as her bed where he placed the paper bag he was carrying.

'Should you wish to go for a swim, I have bought you the necessary,' he told her, and she could see in his unbending attitude that as far as he was concerned the subject of what was to happen before Saturday drew to a close was finished, and that he was adamant she should never bring it up again—only acquiesce.

She didn't thank him for the swimsuit. Knowing she would never wear it, she had no curiosity at all to want to peer inside the bag and enquire his choice.

'You packed in such a hurry,' he went on, apparently not requiring her thanks, 'that you forgot to pack your cosmetics.' He indicated the paper bag. 'I purchased a lipstick and cream that should tide you over. If the colour is all wrong, it will at least save the sun's rays from drying your mouth.'

Unspeaking, Clare stayed where she was, and with one more stern look her way Lazar departed. She waited only for the door to close before she unceremoniously pushed the paper bag to the floor and sank down on the bed.

Not for one moment did she think it thoughtful of him to get into his car and go to collect the items he thought she couldn't do without. All that penetrated her mind was that when she eventually went to him he didn't want to have to place his sensuous mouth over the dry, cracked lips of hers.

Oh, what was she to do? she thought in vain. Even supposing she could bear to worry her parents, there was no way she could get in touch with them either by letter or phone so that they could come to her aid.

She stayed in her room for the next hour, her thoughts going round and around in her head until she thought they would drive her crazy. She had to get out of this room or she would go mad, she thought, and got to her feet only to stand on the paper bag she had an hour earlier knocked from the bed. A spurt of anger moved her to kick it across the room, only to vanish as her natural instinct for tidiness had her going over to pick it up.

Once she had the paper bag in her hands, she found she did have a curiosity after all, and she emptied the contents out on to the bed. Lazar had bought her two swimsuits, not one as she had supposed, she saw. Though the scrap of a thing that was a bikini could hardly be called decent, let alone a swimsuit. The other, though, was much more presentable, being a modest all-in-one affair in a deep shade of brown. It was a regulation swimsuit that had definitely been designed for the purpose of swimming.

She threw it down, knowing she wasn't going to put it on, and examined the lipstick, a pinky red colour that would go beautifully with her colouring, if she had any intention of wearing that either.

Turning away from the bed, intending to make her exit by the sliding glass door, she caught sight of herself in the dressing table mirror. She looked tall and thin despite the voluminous folds of her dress, she thought, and discovered a curiosity about her own body she had never had before. Stepping away from the mirror she took another step towards going outside when that curiosity tugged at her; held her back. Her eyes went to the swimsuit on the bed. She shrugged, and would again have gone forward, but strangely, didn't move.

Hesitating, she looked at the bed again. Perhaps it wouldn't hurt to try it on? Snatching up the swimsuit, she went into the bathroom to poke her head back round the door a few minutes later as though expecting that during her absence an audience had assembled waiting for her to appear. She knew as she stepped from the bathroom that she was just going to have to satisfy the urge to see what she looked like, and hesitation behind her, she went swiftly to the wardrobe, opening the door to get the full length effect in the long mirror appended to the other side of the wardrobe door.

A gasp of astonishment left her when she saw that she stripped off very well. Slightly embarrassed, she forced the feeling down, and stayed to see that, regulation swimsuit or not, it made the best of her firm high bust, even showed an inch or two of cleavage. Quickly she lowered her eyes, glad she had a flat stomach. She had never before realised that she had such long shapely legs either and was surprised to find she was glad she didn't have tree-trunk legs.

Her inspection of her body over, she looked at her face, her silvery hair, darker brows and serious brown eyes, and the impulse was on her to experiment with the lipstick. Other girls began experimenting with make-up before they were fourteen, she knew that, but at fourteen her head had been crammed with so many other things, she recalled, and after fourteen—— She shut her mind off; she didn't want to think about that terrifying winter's night when she had been walking up that dark lane near her home with nothing more on her mind than how pleased her mother would be with the book she had managed to get her from the mobile library.

She saw she had applied too much lipstick and blotted the surplus off with a tissue, flushing the tissue down the lavatory when she went back into the bathroom to get changed into the clothes she was more accustomed to.

Her dress was the first thing to hand, and it seemed to her then as she picked it up that another person had entered her being from the person she knew herself to be. It was that same person who had had her hesitating before trying on the swimsuit; that person who now had her dropping her dress over her head on top of the swimsuit. And then she was outside before the old Clare Harper could have her turning back to her room to change.

She kept her eyes skinned to check that Lazar was not about. She had tried to get through to him and had failed miserably—she wanted no further conversation with him.

It was hot on the beach, but so satisfying to have the whole of it to herself. Drawn to the water's edge, she walked a hundred yards or so along, some sense of calm coming to her as she drank in the beauty of her surroundings, then had to stop as her sandals kept gritting with sand. Her sandals off, she didn't bother to put them on again—pointless anyway; she could spend the whole of the morning extracting sand from them. The sun was hot overhead, the sand hot beneath her feet, making her instinctively head for the water.

It was sheer delight to have the sea lapping her toes and before long she was paddling further in, picking up her dress to her knees to avoid wetting the hem. If only she could swim, she thought, never having been bothered by her lack of prowess in the water before.

Wouldn't it be gorgeous to immerse oneself completely in the cooling waters?

There was nothing to stop her going in chest high though, an inner voice tormented. And suddenly, the new Clare Harper had her going back to the water's edge, taking a very thorough look around to make sure she was still by herself, and then walking further to the beach where she hastily pulled her dress over her head before she could change her mind. From there she ran back to the sea, experiencing fresh delight at another first when with water up to her waist she splashed around and found out how enjoyable such freedom was.

The sun hot on her shoulders, she held her hair on top of her head, wishing she had some pins with which to secure it, then dipped under the water up to her neck, wishing again that she could swim.

Having in part lost herself in the new and enjoyable pastime, she had lost too for the moment the worries that threatened her sanity. And then, for all she knew there was no one about, her selfconsciousness returned, and she wanted only to be out of the water with her dress covering her.

There was an urgency about her as she turned to head for the beach, and the sea was about waist-high when, searching for where she had left her dress, she felt a shaft of horror pierce through her. For there standing watching her was Lazar Vardakas!

Her nerves bundled together in a knot of apprehension and she knew the greatest reluctance to leave the water. And yet she felt far more vulnerable where she was, for he seemed to have taken up a permanent stance and didn't look to be going anywhere. She just couldn't go back to splashing around with him watching.

In a mind to get to the beach as quickly as possible, to get into her dress as rapidly as she could, she realised as she walked towards him that since her dress lay some yards behind him, she would have to go near him.

She might have achieved her aim to get to her dress with some dignity had she not chanced to raise her eyes to his face when a few yards only separated them. But the look in his eyes as he admired her figure had a blush breaking over her which she thought must reach right down to her toes.

Unashamedly his eyes roved from the top of her white cloud of hair, over her bare shoulders and slowly down over her body, her long shapely legs and down to her feet, to return as though attracted by her wet clinging swimsuit, to her breasts. Her eyes followed his, and looking down to her bust line she blushed afresh that the twin peaks of each swelling curve had hardened from the contact with the water and were now standing out for him to see she was very much a woman.

'Stop looking at me like that!' was wrenched from her, and, unable to bear his scrutiny, she made to dart past him. She found Lazar had moved too, and as she reached for her dress, her attempt was thwarted as he picked it up and withheld it from her.

Her attempt at dignity a thing of the past, her dismay would have had her lunging for it, only his voice, speaking coolly, stopped her.

'Why are you so ashamed of your body?' he asked, his eyes going over her again, though she doubted he had missed anything the first time.

'I'm not,' she said tautly.

'Yes, you are,' he dismissed her answer. 'I have seen you in nothing but dresses you could wrap around your slender shape three, maybe four times.'

'I like loose-fitting clothes,' she defended. 'Anyway, I can wear what I like—it's nothing to do with you.'

'I knew you wouldn't wear the bikini when I bought it,' he ignored her defence, 'yet I was sure you had something underneath all that material you cover yourself up with that would be worth seeing.'

Clare didn't want this personal conversation about her body, wanted to get him off the subject. But apparently he was more interested in what went on inside her.

'Your body is beautiful,' he went on, to her growing distress. 'You should be proud to possess so much loveliness. You ...'

But Clare had heard enough. Anxious to get herself covered up, she made a grab for her dress, caught off balance when he moved out of the way, and her trepidation grew as she felt his arms come round her, his hands on her naked back as he saved her from falling.

In that instant, the feel of his hands on her and what could happen if she didn't get away had terror taking over from trepidation, and wildly she pushed at him to be free. Whether or not he liked the feel of her back she didn't have time to decide, but his arms stayed firm around her, refusing to let her go.

She began to shake with dread and managing to get her arms and hands free she hit out at anywhere she could get a blow to land. The sting of her hand across his face had Lazar holding on to her arms, a look of fury coming over his features.

'You hellcat!' he snarled, and as her eyes went wide with fear, he began to haul her up against his hard body.

'No!' she screamed. But there was no one but him to hear her.

Then she was no longer on an isolated beach many miles from her own country. It was not Lazar who held her. She was struggling, fighting to get away from the beast who was intent on violating her body. She was in a dark lane, was being suffocated with nightmare remembrances from the past. The sun had gone; the world was grey.

'No!' she tried to scream, but no sound left her throat as her grey world changed to black, and she fainted.

CHAPTER FOUR

SLOWLY some light began to enter Clare's dark world. Her long lashes fluttered open and she found she was still on the beach, Lazar still with her. Only now where the sun had been hot upon her, she was lying in the shade. He must have carried her there, she thought, her mind clearing and everything that had happened coming back to her.

Wanting to be on her feet and away from him as fast as she could, she struggled to sit up only to find those hands were assisting her.

'Take your hands off me!' she muttered tightly, that familiar alarm starting off again.

Lazar let her go, but she was still weak from her faint and didn't trust her legs to hold her, and the last thing she wanted was to collapse on top of him if her legs crumpled. She concentrated on trying to keep calm for the next few minutes while waiting for her strength to return. Lazar had released her when she had asked him to, so perhaps he wasn't the type to take advantage of her weakened state.

Silently they sat there on the beach, Lazar not saying anything until he saw her faint colour had returned and that she had recovered. Then Clare, about to get to her feet, was stopped by the brusque, unsympathetic:

'Would you mind telling me what the hell all that was about?'

'I—er—fainted,' she replied, not looking at him, resolved to tell him nothing. Nothing would get her telling a soul of those remembrances that had triggered off her faint.

'I know damn well you fainted,' he said shortly, reminding her, 'I was there.' Clare made to get to her feet, anxiously looking around for her dress, but without ceremony he pushed her down again. 'You are going nowhere, Miss Clare Harper, until you tell me exactly what it is about being in my arms that made you pass out like that.'

He was too shrewd by far, Clare thought, her mind searching feverishly for some excuse that would be believable. He had discerned that being in a man's arms frightened the wits out of her, and much though she would like to ask him to pass her dress over so she could cover herself up, there was a greater urgency in her that decreed he should not take that as another indication that she was afraid of men. For over the years a feeling of shame had grown up alongside the feeling of degradation at having been singled out for that vicious attack on her person that dreadful dark night.

Lazar appeared to be in no hurry for her answer. He looked in fact to be ready to wait all day exactly where they were for her to string her words together. And as a cold sweat broke out on her body, Clare knew with a sort of hysterical conviction that if her answer didn't satisfy him, he might well embrace her again if that was the only way to get the answers he wanted.

'It had nothing to do with being—in your arms that made me faint,' she said at last.

'No?' He didn't sound convinced.

'No.'

'You are telling me you weren't terrified a while ago? That you didn't fight as though you thought I wasn't going to wait until Saturday to claim retribution for Sophronia?'

'I didn't want that to happen, but you've known that all along,' she said. 'Good heavens,'—was that she who gave a mocking laugh to accompany those two words? She chalked up amateur actress to her other newly discovered talents—'girls no longer swoon when a man makes a grab for them,' she scoffed.

He looked sharply at her, causing her to feel better that it looked as though this was more what he believed in in an Englishwoman.

'It's the heat,' she went on, desperation having its reward as the idea popped into her head. 'I'm not used to it. I expect I've been out in the sun too long, and that plus—er—grappling with you must have sapped my strength.'

His eyes narrowed as he looked at her, and she wished she knew what was going on inside his head. For a long moment he considered her, his voice almost silky when next it came.

'So—you are telling me that you do not fear anything to do with men?'

'Of course not,' she said stoutly, and even managed another scoffing laugh, only for it to fade, a sick feel-

ing entering her stomach when Lazar stood up, looked
her over casually and said:

'Good. In that case I need not have any qualms about
the way we shall come together.' His mouth was smiling a deceptive smile when he drawled, 'Don't stay
too long out here. It doesn't appear to be too good for
you.'

Clare sat a while longer when he had gone, feeling
more herself now she was on her own, her mind busy
with everything that had gone on. Her brow wrinkled
as she tried to find hidden meanings in their conversation. Last night Lazar had been disbelieving that she
had never had a boy-friend. Was he now believing,
with her saying she feared nothing with men, that what
she was actually telling him was that she was not a
virgin? He knew quite well she didn't want to go to
bed with him, so had he taken from the fact she had
hit out at him that, virgin though she had led him to
believe she was not, she liked to pick and choose her
own affairs, and not have them thrust upon her?

She made her way back to the villa and once in her
room had Lazar taken temporarily from her mind as
she found that the clothes she had worn up until last
night had without her knowing it been taken away by
Phoebe and were now sitting washed and ironed on her
bed.

How kind it was of her, she thought, yet she could
have done with having something to do. She wouldn't
at all have minded giving a hand with the housework,
for all Phoebe seemed to manage very well without her
help. She knew before she asked that any offer of assist-
ance she made would be refused, not only that but
would be frowned upon by the lord and master.

Listlessly she went to get out of her swimsuit, to shower and dress and to rinse out the swimsuit, knowing she would never wear it again.

For the rest of the day she stayed in her room. She just couldn't face seeing her host again and since she was completely without appetite when Phoebe came to tell her lunch was ready, she signed to her that she wasn't feeling well and didn't want any. It was a lie that she wasn't feeling well. But since Lazar had been there when she fainted, had been the cause of it, she thought it was an excuse he couldn't argue against.

Her tummy was rumbling when the long hours of the afternoon wore on to dinner time. But the thought of having to face Lazar Vardakas across the dining room table had her certain she didn't want any dinner either.

It was shortly after seven that evening as she lay on her bed, concentrating on ignoring the hungry pleas of her stomach, that, again without knocking, the door to her room opened and Lazar Vardakas stood there.

Moving to a sitting position, Clare stared fixedly at him as he came near and perched himself on the edge of her bed.

'How are you feeling now?' he asked, and she was surprised to hear a gentle note in his voice, as though he was really concerned that his kidnap victim was indisposed.

'Better,' she found herself saying, when it had been in her mind to play the invalid way past the hour of vengeance.

'Good,' he said briefly, his eyes checking her face for his own satisfaction. 'In view of your absence at lunch, I have had dinner brought forward. We shall eat in about half an hour.'

'I'm not hungry,' she said quickly, and watched as all sign of gentleness left him and his face went deadly cold.

'You will eat,' he commanded, and looking over her crumpled dress with disdain, 'Go now and wash and change. You will feel better still once you have freshened up.'

'I don't ...' she began, only to receive a blast of more of his insufferable arrogance, his haughty look stopping her.

'I am quite able to act the lady's maid myself if need be,' he told her meaningfully. And Clare knew then that if she wasn't at the dinner table in half an hour, he would return to dunk her in the bath, haul her out, then dry and dress her.

Defeated, she glared at him, her temper this time lasting for more than three seconds as it got her over his intimidating arrogance.

'Oh, go away!' she snapped aggressively. 'I'm fed up to the teeth with you and your bossy pronouncements!'

Mutiny in every line of her, she got up from the bed on the other side, and was even more infuriated when instead of making him lose his cool, she took a look at him and saw from his wide grin that her tantrum had amused him. Without another word she went into the bathroom and viciously slammed the door.

Of course her temper didn't last. And as she rapidly cooled down she was once more amazed at herself that she had let fly at him as she had. She had no thought to get out of her clothes until she heard the outer door close. When it did she returned to the bedroom to select fresh underwear and take one of her newly washed dresses from the wardrobe.

By the time she was ready to join Lazar, she was back

to being afraid again. Soon it would be dark, and she hated the night-time. It made the fate that awaited her take on proportions she could just about cope with during the day, but which at night had her dread growing with every sleepless hour.

As a result, she only pecked at her food, delicious though it was, and included the dolmades, vine leaves stuffed with rice soaked in oil, which she had heard of but had never tasted. But what she did eat satisfied her stomach, the veal that followed being superbly cooked. She refused Lazar's offer to peel her a piece of fruit at the end of the meal, wondering if all the tenseness in the atmosphere came from her—or did Lazar have a share of it too? For unlike last night, he had spoken very little, and was obviously in no mind to draw her out further.

'Can I go now?' she asked, when she saw his coffee cup was empty, her nerves on the point of cracking.

For her trouble she received a sour look that she was hiding under a cloak of politeness to tell him she found his company unbearable.

Then suddenly into the tense stillness a telephone shrilled. Clare jumped, startled, the sound was so unexpected. She looked at Lazar and with the phone still ringing had a tailor-made excuse for leaving him. She blamed her bad luck that if she had waited a few seconds she could have gone to her room without receiving one of his disfavouring looks—though she was at a loss to know why it should bother her how he looked at her.

'You'll want to take your call privately,' she said, getting up from the table.

His glance was sardonic. 'Since I shall most likely be

speaking in Greek, I doubt that any business secrets will be leaked.'

Clare turned, ready to march back to her room, only to find he was right there at her elbow. In a hurry to be away from him, she was further obstructed by Rasmus coming to stand in the doorway telling Lazar who was on the phone, not a word of which did she understand. When Rasmus moved out of the way, she again went to go forward, knowing Lazar was keeping pace with her, but anticipating that she would be free of him when they reached the door which she thought to be his study.

The door stood open, obviously left so by Rasmus. About to pass it, Clare caught a glimpse of a large desk and knew she was right in her surmise that this must be where Lazar shut himself away to get on with some work when she couldn't see him around.

His hand on her arm jerked her to a halt, turning her and causing her to look up enquiringly at him. And what he said then had all her alarms for herself sinking into obscurity, for what he said was:

'I was wrong in my surmise that I was about to discuss a business matter.' And while she stared uncomprehendingly, casually he added, 'My brother Aeneas is waiting to speak with me.' He let go of her arm to go striding into the study, promptly picking up the phone and speaking in his own language.

But if he thought he could give her that piece of information and leave her to go to her room without enquiring what Aeneas, her brother's jailor, had to say, then he was very much mistaken. Without waiting for an invitation, Clare followed him into the room, knowing he was aware she was there, for all his flow of Greek remained uninterrupted.

There was a pause at Lazar's end of the conversation, and she saw his eyes sweep over her as he listened to what his brother was saying. Then he was saying something that sounded very much like a command and had all her instincts knowing that he had asked to speak to Kit.

It was confirmed for her a moment later when without her ears needing to pick up that Lazar had switched to English, she saw his face grow hard, the look in his eyes icy cold. And though his tones were controlled, she sensed there was a raging anger boiling beneath the surface as she heard him say tightly, clearly interrupting whatever it was Kit was explaining:

'Just tell me "Yes" or "No"—did you take my sister back with you to that apartment?'

What Kit answered Clare had no way of knowing, but she was certain he hadn't limited his reply to either a positive or negative answer, for suddenly a savage Lazar was blazing into him.

'How *dare* you attempt to blacken my sister's name by suggesting she has lied?' He sliced through Kit again when he tried to get a word in. 'I have no need to question her. She would not lie to her parents, of that I am convinced.' Then before Kit could utter more than one word, Lazar's flaming temper had changed to biting ice as with freezing coldness he told him, 'You have taken my sister to your bed for sufficient time to remove her virtue. Permit me to tell you I have *your* sister, Clare, here with me. She will be treated in exactly the same way as you treated Sophronia.'

White-faced, Clare could only stand and stare, her whole being numb at the hard, ruthless way Lazar had informed Kit of what he intended to do to her. She watched as though in slow motion as Lazar pulled the phone away from his ear as an offensive barrage of rage screamed from Kit at the other end.

And then, after for so long being the one who had always been so protected, she felt something inside her snap, and she had wrenched the phone out of Lazar's hand, and it was she who was the one who was doing the protecting.

'It's all right Kit, it's all right,' she tried to soothe him down.

'How in God's name did he get you there?' Kit was saying, making a superhuman effort to get over his shock. 'And where the hell is Bruce? Has that swine ... Oh God ... I'm so bloody helpless stuck on this island with no way to get to you!'

'I'm fine,' Clare continued to soothe, tears coming to her eyes as she heard the dreadful anxiety for her in Kit's voice. 'For all he says, Lazar has been a perfect gentleman.' Kit sounded ready to go off his head if she couldn't make him believe he had no cause to be upset.

'He hasn't—touched you?'

'No, no, of course not. I'm being treated very well. It's more like a holiday than anything else,' she said, hoping she could finish this conversation without breaking down. Kit would never believe her if he heard her crying. 'Don't worry, Kit,' she said, and tried to reassure him, 'You have nothing to worry about, I promise you ...'

A Greek voice came into her ear, and she guessed the phone had been taken away from Kit. Without looking at Lazar she handed him the phone, heard him terminate the call and saw the receiver go down.

Only then did she look up, and her glance met his head-on. She couldn't look away from that ice cold look.

'So,' he queried softly, 'you have told your brother he has no need to worry on your behalf.' Clare didn't answer. She felt used up, incapable of speech. Then Lazar's voice came again, softly still, yet with an added threatening sound to it. 'It isn't the done thing to lie to members of one's own family,' he said, in a way that made all her senses tingle. 'But just in case you are in any doubt about your position here, perhaps I should tell you that if your brother isn't worried on your behalf,' his voice dropped the soft note, 'then he damn well should be!' Clare didn't wait to hear any more. She fled.

Strangely, as she lay in bed that night, her fears for her own safety mingling with anguish over what Kit must be going through now that he knew she was here in Greece without any one member from her family looking out for her, it wasn't either her mother or her father, Bruce or Kit whose face came to mind just before sleep took her, but the face of Lazar Vardakas and the way he had looked when he had grinned after she had fired up at him before dinner. He had looked so much younger then, free from care, happy, likeable. On that oddest of thoughts she drifted into sleep, and for the first time since Saturday, the first night in her home alone, she had a good night's sleep.

Barely able to believe she had slept through the night without once waking, Clare opened her eyes to see it was daylight, though there was no sun this morning. A fine drizzle had set in, but that didn't particularly bother her. She always felt better in the daylight, and though Kit occupied many of her thoughts as she showered and dressed, the situation didn't seem quite so threatening as it had last night.

Breakfast on the terrace was out this morning, that

much was obvious. Feeling hungry, Clare left her room, and came across Phoebe, who showed her into a breakfast room that had a breathtaking panoramic view of the pine woods.

Clare had barely started to eat when Lazar appeared. But this morning, to her puzzlement, seeing him in no way affected her appetite. He greeted her morosely, she thought, and went to stare out of the window at the drizzling rain.

While his back was to her she had ample opportunity to study him, dressed as he was in dark trousers and a body-hugging shirt. The breadth of his shoulders was remarkable in such a lean man, she found herself thinking, hastily averting her eyes and concentrating on her toast as he tired of the view and turned. She felt his eyes on her, guessed from his moody silence that she wasn't his favourite person this morning, and got the shock of her life when he said, his voice not very encouraging:

'Finish your breakfast, I'll take you for a drive.'

'Drive!' She raised her eyes from her plate and saw he was staring back at her with a 'take it or leave it' attitude.

'The idea doesn't appeal to you?'

'Well, yes—but . . .'

The idea did appeal. Exploring the grounds or wandering along the beach would be out in this weather, and the thought of spending hours shut in her room as she had done yesterday suddenly was not to be borne. Yet she was suspicious of him. Why should he want to take her driving? It wasn't as though he liked her enough to want to spend time enclosed in a car with her.

'Why?' she asked. 'If you want to go driving you have no need to take me along.'

He made no pretence of being polite. 'Let's just say I thought you might like to see something of the country in which you find yourself.' He was obviously fed up. 'But you can please yourself. I shall be leaving in half an hour.' He strode past her then, leaving her to her solitary breakfast.

Ten minutes later as she tidied her hair in her room, she tried to tell herself she was only going with him because she knew he didn't really want her to go with him, tried to tell herself it was only because she knew it would niggle him when she presented herself for the excursion, and could see no reason why, since he had put the fear of God in her, she shouldn't make him suffer a little too.

But when she placed herself at the window of the terrace where he couldn't fail to see her if he drove the car to the front of the villa, she knew it was because he had sparked her interest in suggesting she might like to see something of his country.

She saw him bring the Mercedes to the front of the terrace, saw the soft top had been put in place to protect them from the rain, and knew anxiety just in case he failed to spot her standing there. The rain had given over for the moment, but she thought it likely it would soon start up again.

Lazar got out of the car, seemed to be checking something to do with the soft top, then catching Clare by surprise he raised his eyes to where she was waiting. For a second or two he just stood watching her, then with an indication of his hand he motioned for her to join him.

For the first half hour of the drive a tense silence filled the car. Perhaps it was only tension on her part, Clare thought, as she tried to relax, but Lazar wasn't helping by maintaining a moody silence. Not that she wanted him to say anything to her. Heaven forbid! she thought, putting all her concentration into enjoying the mountainous terrain they were going through. It was magnificent scenery and she only wished she felt less strung up and more able to enjoy it. Then she noticed that the rain she had thought had set in for the rest of the day was holding off.

'It looks as though it may clear up,' she remarked, more because she was feeling the strain of the heavy silence getting through to her than anything else.

Lazar didn't answer, and she was just thinking 'Oh, get on with it, then' when after negotiating a tight bend in the road, he replied:

'I hoped it might. I'll take the top off later if the weather continues to improve.'

Was that an indication that they would be out for longer than just a spin? Clare felt some of her tenseness leave her. He had bothered to answer her after all, so perhaps he wasn't being as moody as she had supposed.

A half an hour later he steered the car into the fishing port of Moudania, driving through the town square with its huge plane tree and to the harbour, where he stopped the car.

'Like to stretch your legs?' he suggested, turning to her with a pleasant look on his face, which made her wonder how she had ever thought him morose and moody.

'Please.' Already her hand was going to the door catch on her side.

What time the fishing boats had gone out, or come in for that matter, she had no idea, but she was fascinated to stand and observe the fishing vessels, all of which seemed to be festooned with lights which they must switch on when they were out to sea.

Standing there, she was aware of tourists going back and forth, her ears easily picking up English voices. And then she saw a boat that wasn't a fishing vessel but a small yacht with a Union Jack flying from its mast, and suddenly her heart lightened, her tensions disappeared completely, and she turned to Lazar who had been standing patiently by her side, and smiled.

For a few seconds there was no reaction from him. Then as his eyes followed the direction hers had gone, observing as she had done her country's flag, he turned his attention back to her.

'Does seeing that make you feel homesick?'

Clare thought about it for a moment. No, it hadn't made her feel homesick. It had lifted her, made her feel less alien in a country that was not her own, had given her a feeling of happiness almost—yet strangely, not homesickness.

'No,' she said honestly, and left it at that. Then she felt the most peculiar sensation in her heart region when Lazar looked pleased, and he too smiled.

I must have eaten my breakfast too quickly, Clare thought, dismissing the peculiar feeling she had received when he had smiled. She had rather hurried with her toast, wanting to make sure he didn't leave without her.

After that the day picked up in more ways than just the weather. It was as though her telling him she wasn't homesick had eased any constraint he was feeling. Almost at once the tension between them fell away and Lazar even teased her when she showed an interest in the local taverna, suggesting she wanted to be like the other tourists and sample one.

'Will they be open?' she asked.

For answer he took charge of her elbow and guided her across the street, where they sat outside a taverna and drank coffee before going back to the car where after one look at the cloudless blue sky, Lazar took the top off the Mercedes.

Perhaps it was because she was among different scenery that she found the experience of sitting beside Lazar while they sped along so exhilarating. Not that he was going all that fast, for he seemed to think she should look her fill at the superb views about her. Yes, that was it. It was the scenery that made her feel so alive, she thought, for she had often been a passenger in Kit's open-topped car and had never felt like this.

Any heat that would have scorched her was absorbed by the breeze the car created, lifting her hair and bring ing a glow to her cheeks as her eyes feasted on everything there was to see.

Small shrines appeared at every road junction. She was fascinated to see white blobs of cotton growing in fields as they passed, some already having been harvested, and astonished when in the middle of nowhere, some enterprising watermelon grower had set up a stall clearly hoping to do business with anyone who would stop.

A house or two appeared, and as she saw a stationary aircraft, she thought this must be where she and Lazar had landed. Her assumption proved correct when Lazar told her they were entering Thessaloniki, adding that they would lunch there. She told him, quite relaxed now and oddly feeling in no way threatened by him, that she preferred the Greek name for Greece's second city, rather than the plain-sounding translation, Salonika, and was rewarded by a little snippet when he told her:

'Thessaloniki was the sister of Alexander the Great. It is said the city was named after her.'

History had always been a favourite of Clare's, and it was without any thought of showing off her knowledge that she said, 'Alexander, king of the Macedonians,' and received a grin from Lazar that made her glad she had decided to come with him.

Once he had parked the car, Clare realised she couldn't lunch anywhere with her hair so blown about, and rooted about in her bag, only to find she had left her comb back on the dressing table.

'I've forgotten my comb,' she mourned, her latent femininity stirring.

Lazar looked at her, and she felt a flutter of panic when his head came nearer, only for that panic to die when he searched in a compartment on her side, ran a comb to earth and handed it to her with the comment, 'Sophronia's.'

Clare used Sophronia's comb, musing while she did so that that was the first time he had mentioned his sister's name in her hearing without that hard edge of anger to his voice.

They lunched in the smartest hotel she had ever been in. That it wasn't Lazar's first visit and that his was a respected name was obvious not only by the first-class treatment they received, but by the way he was addressed. The waiter answering in English when because of her presence Lazar addressed him in her mother tongue.

Since she had stated she would prefer to try a Greek

meal and ignore the many steaks offered, Lazar guided her choice over taramosalata, a fish roe pâté, which was so delicious she could have made a meal of that on its own without the pastichio which followed and consisted of macaroni with minced meat in a sauce with parmesan cheese.

Lazar conversed easily with her over lunch, and if occasionally he brought a shy smile to her lips that had him staring at her longer than usual, she was entirely unaware of the reason. All she was aware of was that somehow he had her talking in return, she who was always most reserved with strangers.

At one stage he referred to her knowing Alexander the Great had been king of Macedonia, seeming surprised that she knew too Alexander had in his early teens been a pupil of the great philosopher Aristotle himself.

'We are not far from Alexander's birthplace,' he informed her, adding to her enormous delight, 'The archaeologists have been excavating the remains of his palace for some years now. Would you like to see it?'

Her eyes were positively shining when she squeaked, 'Could we?'

He grinned at her obvious awe, and Clare felt that peculiar sensation in her heart region again, and realised she had made a pig of herself with the taramosalata.

Lazar nodded. 'But first I think perhaps we should walk off our lunch.'

The heat when they went outside the air-conditioned hotel met them fiercely, and Clare had no idea what Lazar's intention was when he took hold of her arm and piloted her into one of the local shops.

That was until he stopped with her at one counter

and with a babble of every language under the sun
going on around her, she was made sharply aware of
him when he took from the assistant who had hurried
to do his bidding a classy-looking stiff linen sun hat and
promptly placed the tall crown with its snappy brim
on her head.

'Goētevtikos,' he said, standing back to admire the
angle at which he had placed it on her head.

Clare didn't know what the word meant, but the way
he had said it sounded so much like a compliment that
she blushed and was glad at that moment he turned
away to pay the attending assistant, also affording her
the chance to get a peep at herself in the mirror.

With astonishment she observed how different she
looked—from the neck up, anyway. Her style of dress
she was used to, though she found she was wishing with
a longing foreign to her that she had something different to wear. She rejected such yearnings, knowing she
was quite happy with her present wardrobe, and concentrated on her hat. It made her look—how? Not
sophisticated, she doubted she would ever be that, but
certainly as though there was more to her than the
shy awkward female she had been to date.

'Didn't you believe me when I said you looked
charming?'

Lazar's voice brought her eyes instantly away from
the mirror. She refrained from telling him he had
spoken in Greek before, as this time she couldn't hope
to hide from him the fact that she had blushed again.

Happily pacing along beside him, she had no idea
where he was taking her once they had left the shop.
She was getting more used to the heat now, but when
he took her inside a beautiful Byzantine church and

allowed her to satiate her eyes, she felt the air almost cold in contrast to the heat outside.

The church had only recently been repaired, he told her, many of such buildings having suffered when Thessaloniki had experienced an earthquake some years before.

Her excitement began to mount when they went back to the car. Soon they would be at Pella, Alexander's birthplace; she could hardly wait to see it. Before leaving Thessaloniki, as she preferred to call it, they passed an interesting-looking round tower, and wanting to cram in as much as she could, she asked what it was.

'It is called The White Tower,' Lazar informed her, going on to tell her how it was illuminated at night, but adding, 'I am afraid we are not able to see round it. It is only open for ten days of the year and that is when the International Fair is held here, but that will not be until next month.'

Why, when she was so anxious to get home, back to the safety her family provided, she should suddenly feel regretful that come September she would be far away from Greece, Clare could not understand. But it seemed to cast a blight on the day, a blight which was not relieved until Lazar had driven to a plain, in the middle of which Pella was situated.

The archaeologists had done their work well in uncovering a palace that had been built more than two thousand years ago, Clare thought, as without haste she and Lazar walked round the site examining tall ridged pillars and floor mosaics. The mosaics were made from thousands of tiny evenly matched pebbles. It must have taken an army of artists a lifetime, she thought in wonder, thrilled into silence, grateful that Lazar was letting her take it all in without saying a word.

At last she had to come away, but her mind was so full of what she had seen, when she stumbled into him not realising he had halted to let an elderly matron go in front of them, it was an instinctive gesture to hold on to his arm. And just as instinctive when she realised what she had done to try and pull her hand away. But she found Lazar must like the feel of her hand in the crook of his arm, for he instructed:

'Leave it there.' And when her heart began to beat hurriedly, he added casually, 'There is some uneven ground, you might fall.' Then just as casually he told her, 'There are a few more mosaics in a small museum across the road. Would you like to take a look?'

Once inside the museum, he allowed her to let go of his arm so that she could wander at will round the treasures it held, though he came and stood by her when she reached the most impressive in her view of all the mosaics. It depicted a man either side of a lion, done in the tiny pebbles she had seen a short while ago, and she listened with rapt attention as Lazar told her it was thought the man wearing the hat was Alexander himself, the bareheaded figure that of Krateros, who had saved Alexander's life in a lion hunt.

When they left Pella she knew they would now be making for the villa. But the thought did not disturb her as much as it should have done, and she realised then, with utter amazement, that against all odds of it being so, she had just spent one of the happiest days of her life.

They broke their journey back to call at one of the secluded holiday hotels en route where they had tea, a silence settling between them when they went back to the car. Clare felt tired, but that wasn't the reason for her being so quiet, she thought in confusion. How could she have been so happy when Kit ...

'You are feeling well, Clare?' Lazar enquired, when it must have come to him that some time had gone by without her saying anything.

'I'm fine,' she answered, and thought he must be tired too after his many hours of driving, for after that he had little to say either. And then he was turning the car down the drive to the villa.

Clare quickly hopped out, feeling shy suddenly, for all she had conversed so freely with him for most of the day. 'Thank you very much for today, Lazar.' She spoke politely, and as he looked back at her, his face once more severe now that they were at his home where the time he had allotted her to come to him was fast dwindling, her shyness overcame every other thought and she turned and bolted indoors.

Closing the door of her room, she leaned hard against it for several seconds. Then taking off the hat Lazar had purchased for her, she stared at it, her mind going from him to all that was wonderful she had seen that day. And she knew then that northern Greece had stolen part of her heart.

CHAPTER FIVE

WHEN Clare awoke the next morning, she notched up another satisfactory night's sleep. She wondered how that was possible, because she had more than enough on her mind to keep her awake for hours, and yet no sooner had she closed her eyes than she had floated off into sleep.

All that fresh air, I expect, she thought, as she got out of bed and without enthusiasm selected the dress she was going to wear.

Lazar was nowhere to be seen when she went to the terrace for her breakfast, and as she felt relief wash over her that this was so, she realised she was shy of seeing him again after the magic of yesterday, in case he had changed back to the cold hard man he sometimes was.

He hadn't put in an appearance at dinner last night either, she mused as she sipped her fruit juice. The thought that had slipped into her mind while eating her dinner alone the night before came again. Had he not enjoyed the day as much as he appeared to have done? Had he found her company so unstimulating he had had to go out last night and seek more sophisticated company?

She couldn't blame him if he had. After all, he was a man of the world. The small insight he had given her into his life while lunching in Thessaloniki had shown her he jetted everywhere, could be in London one day on business, New York the next. How could she hope to compete with the elegant women, well versed in the art of socialising, he must meet daily?

Her thoughts stopped right there. Compete? Had she actually thought of the word 'compete' in relation to herself, other women and Lazar Vardakas? Good heavens! She wasn't interested in him on a woman-to-man basis! Her only interest in him was that of trying to get Kit free without any dreadful harm befalling him.

But having had the word 'compete' popping into her head, however ridiculous, she was forced to try and discover what had led up to such a change in her thinking.

She was draining the last of her coffee before it came to her that insidiously, without her ever being aware of it, Lazar had been working on her to break down the barrier of her reserve.

Not that he had once stepped out of line. Oh, he had admired her shape when she had revealed herself in a swimsuit. Had made her aware she was a woman. They had wrestled on the beach, but, she realised now, it hadn't been Lazar's intention to kiss her that day she had fainted. It had been her own hysteria, the panic of her imagination; those terrifying remembrances that had done that. He was adamant that she should go to him before Saturday. And tomorrow was Saturday! Familiar panic tried to get started within her, but she battled to keep it down, needing to think her thoughts through with as little emotion getting in the way as could be achieved.

Lazar Vardakas must have observed something in her that told him she would find it impossible to go to him cold. And though he hadn't once yesterday made any physical overture to her—she remembered that moment in the car when she had thought he had been going to kiss her, but that hadn't been his intention at all; he had merely bent over to the compartment that held the comb she required. No, she thought, placing her coffee cup in her saucer, all yesterday had been about was building up a friendly atmosphere. To gain her trust. To get her to unwind—to feel at ease with him—so that tonight when she went to him ...

At that point her mind shied from going any further. She wasn't up to coping with the rest of it, of wondering why Lazar should go to such lengths on her behalf.

It was enough to know that for the sins laid at Kit's door, Lazar was demanding that by tomorrow a price should be paid. His family honour was at stake and he was determined on one thing, that Clare should be the one to pay that price—in full.

While she had been sitting there she had, without noticing it, been aware that Rasmus was in the garden some way away busy with a hose pipe. But for a few seconds her attention became riveted on the section where he was when Lazar appeared from nowhere and went to speak to him.

Whether or not Lazar expected to see her sitting on the terrace, she had no idea, but he couldn't avoid seeing her when he turned his head to where she was sitting. He made a move that looked as though he was going to come over and say something to her, but such a clamour of wild emotions cascaded through her that she was on her feet and disappearing through the terrace doors before he could have taken more than two steps towards her.

As though being chased by Dracula himself, Clare sped along the hall, stopping for nothing when she reached her room, but closing the door behind her and exiting through the sliding window. Rapidly her feet skirted the house, taking a line towards the pine trees she had explored that first day.

She stopped when she reached them, had a good vantage point of the villa from where she stood, and waited but saw no sign of Lazar coming after her. The clamouring inside her settled down, but she was nowhere near ready to leave her hiding place.

A short while later she heard the Mercedes start up, and watched when the car came into view, making out Lazar at the wheel, obviously off somewhere. Well, he hadn't gone out in his boat, Clare thought with relief, and spent the rest of the morning wandering in the pine wood getting herself into a frame of mind where, since she couldn't hope to avoid him for very much longer, she could meet him at lunch with as much equanimity as possible.

But Lazar did not put in an appearance at lunch time, and she wished she knew something of the Greek language so she could subtly question Phoebe as to his whereabouts.

In her room and opening one of the drawers for a fresh handkerchief, Clare spotted the brown swimsuit Lazar had bought for her. Phoebe must have put it away, she realised, and would have closed the drawer again, only the thought came—if Lazar intended to be out all day, and since he hadn't returned for his meal that must be the case, she would have the whole of the beach to herself for the rest of the afternoon. It was scorchingly hot out. She thought lovingly of those refreshing sea waters, then thought no more until she had her dress on over the top of her swimsuit and the warm sand beneath her feet.

She walked along the beach sandals in hand, glad of the sun hat Lazar had purchased for her yesterday as the sun beat down. Thinking to let her lunch settle before she made any excursion into the water, she found a spot of shade and sat down to let her thoughts wander.

They weren't allowed to wander very far. For as she looked back to the villa her pulses leapt to see that not only had Lazar returned, but he was walking her way. Her first instinct to get to her feet and flee had to be stifled. She couldn't spend all day running away from him. Besides, he must already think her markedly different from the other sort of women he knew. Not that she wanted to be like them, of course she didn't.

She watched him approach, tall, athletic, easy-striding. He must have driven up while she had the taps on washing her hands, for she hadn't heard his car. He halted when he was only a yard from her, causing her to crane her neck to look up at him, her speech temporarily suspended; she could think of nothing to say.

'Hello, Clare Harper,' he said in that barely accented voice. 'Mind if I join you?' He didn't wait for her assent, but dropped to the sand beside her.

'I thought I saw—heard you go out,' she said, knew she had muffed it, and looked in an opposite direction, feeling a blush coming on.

'You did,' he said, not commenting on the 'saw' or 'heard' part of her statement. 'I came looking for you to see if you would like to come with me, but you weren't in your room.'

'I ...' she began, trying to think up something that would make her seem less gauche to him than she must already appear, only to find she had no need as he continued:

'Not that it would have proved all that interesting. You would have had to wait around while I did a few necessary jobs for my uncle, but you might have enjoyed the drive.'

'Uncle?'

Clare picked on the one word that might take him away from asking why she had run off the way she had. And Lazar went on to explain that he had received a telephone call before dinner last night to say his uncle had met with a car accident which had necessitated him dropping everything to get to the hospital at once.

'I apologise for leaving you to dine alone,' he ended courteously.

But the fact she had dined alone was not important to Clare then as her natural sympathy had her forgetting the thoughts and feelings that had disturbed her.

'Your uncle—is he going to be all right?' she enquired gently.

'Oh yes. He was looking a little the worse for wear when I saw him last night, but even so,' he said, looking slightly amused, 'nothing can stop the old fellow being a business man first and a hospital patient second. Sedated as he was, it didn't hinder him giving me a whole list of telephone calls I must make on his behalf or business documents I must take for him to look through this morning.'

Clare had to smile too as she visualised a shrewd old man, sick as he must be, still determined not to let the grass grow under his feet.

'He was better when you saw him today?'

'You could say he was giving them hell,' Lazar said with a grin she suddenly found fascinating.

Hastily she looked away, sorting round in her mind for something to say. 'Er—you have relatives in northern Greece, then?' she brought out, and could have groaned at the stupidity of her remark. It was obvious he had.

But if Lazar thought her remark stupid he didn't say so as he revealed, 'We are a large family. I have relatives all over the place. Though in actual fact we are Macedonians by birthright. While my father's family moved on and went into shipping, my mother's side stayed on in agriculture, textiles, tobacco,' he elucidated, adding, 'Which all works well, since they wouldn't dream of using any other shipping line to

Take this superb volume
FREE!

Return to Tuckarimba by Amanda Doyle. Nonie intended to buy back her childhood home, but Jacey Lomax, the present owner, decided not to sell. So Nonie returned to her home as an employee instead, looking after Jacey's crippled brother, Raynor. Losing her heart to Jacey was pure folly, Nonie realized too late, because Jacey loved Delphine.

Hold Me Captive by Margaret Pargeter. After a heated argument with her sister, Amanda had to get away. But her flight led to great difficulties when she found herself snowbound in the middle of Dartmoor with a disconcerting stranger named Jason Meade. This situation was to prove far more emotionally disturbing than the one she'd just escaped!

Greek Bridal by Henrietta Reid. Stranded in Greece with no money, Christine was grateful for the help of Nicholas Martinos — but it had to stop at gratitude, she told herself firmly. It was inevitable that Nick should marry Mariga, whom he had known all his life. But Christine found she just couldn't keep from caring about Nick...

In the pages of your FREE GIFT Romance Treasury Volume you'll get to know warm, true-to-life people, and you'll discover the special kind of miracle that love can be. The stories will sweep you to distant lands where intrigue, adventure and the destiny of many lives will thrill you. All three full-length novels are exquisitely bound together in a single hardcover volume that's your FREE GIFT, to introduce you to Harlequin Romance Treasury!

The most beautiful books you've ever seen!
Cover and spine of all volumes feature distinctive gilt designs. And an elegant bound-in ribbon bookmark adds a lovely feminine touch. No detail has been overlooked to make Romance Treasury books as beautiful and lasting as the stories they contain. What a delightful way to enjoy the very best and most popular Harlequin romances again and again!

A whole world of romantic adventure! As well as your FREE GIFT volume, you'll also receive a second volume of Romance Treasury novels, three more stories as meaningful and as moving as love itself. If you decide to keep the second volume, you will then be entitled to examine each new volume of Romance Treasury novels as they are published.

If however, you decide not to keep the second volume, simply return it and you'll hear no more. And remember, whatever you decide, the beautiful FREE GIFT VOLUME is yours to keep forever. No obligation to by anything ever! Fill out the coupon today to get your free gift volume.

Romance Treasury
from Harlequin

Three exciting, Harlequin full length Romance novels in one beautiful book...

This superb volume is yours FREE!

« Exciting details inside

Detach and mail post paid card today.

export their merchandise but ours!'

The smile in his voice as he said it had her knowing that in no way did they rely on family loyalties for the majority of their business. Common sense told her they must have dealings all over the world.

Shyly she asked what role he played in the business, and learned that he was in charge of obtaining outside contracts. Which also told her why he had studied in England, since he must have been prepared to take up this specialist work at an early age, and the use of English was of paramount importance when getting contracts from other countries.

'How many languages do you speak?' she asked, following her own line of thought.

'Six or seven,' he replied casually, just as though everybody did. And as her eyes flew wide, aware as she was of her own limitations in that area, he added, 'I think you'll find that most Greeks with any sort of education speak at least three languages.'

Feelings dreadfully ignorant, Clare stared out to sea, the idea with her that when she returned home, somehow she was going to learn to speak another language if she had to rely solely on textbooks to do it. The last years of her schooling had been badly interrupted. It had been over a year before she had returned to school, apart from the time off she had to take on her bad days. But as Lazar carried on, talking naturally with no sign of showing off as he spoke of the two universities he had attended, one in England, one here in Greece, slowly in the peace and quiet of the afternoon Clare got over her feeling of inadequacy about the difference in their educations, realising that even if her school work had suffered, she was still able to follow everything he said and make the occasional comment of her own, so her intelligence had remained unimpaired.

A feeling of being in harmony with him surprised her, so that when Lazar said in an unhurried sort of way, 'Let's go for a swim,' she didn't back away in fright as she would have done only a few days ago, but found she was telling him:

'I'm sorry, I can't. I don't.'

'You mean you can't swim?'

Perhaps it was because there was no sign of amazement in his voice that she didn't sink back into feeling inadequate again. She shook her head. 'I never learned.'

'Then I suggest now is as good a time as any to begin,' he said quietly. And when she just sat and stared at him, 'Go and get your swimsuit on, I'll teach you.'

'You'll teach me!' she exclaimed, a peculiar feeling starting up inside her. Then as his superbly white even teeth showed in a teasing grin at her surprise, which only added to her confusion, she found herself telling him, 'Ac-actually, I have my swimsuit on.'

'Then *actually*,' he teased in a swanky English accent, 'let's go to it!'

A smile started within her at his teasing, but it didn't get to appear as without more ado he unbuttoned his shirt to drop it casually down on the sand near her. She looked hastily away when he began to undo his trousers, then heard the roar of his amused laughter when he said:

'I seldom bathe in the nude when women are present.'

Her eyes flicked to him to see he was out of his trousers and was wearing the briefest of black swimming trunks. Her heart racing, she saw the tanned breadth of his uncovered shoulders, his chest bare except for the mat of dark hair that marched down to his navel, then began again. Hurriedly Clare flipped her eyes to his straight legs, his muscled thighs, and she blushed crimson when her eyes flicked up to his and she saw he had observed she had been surveying him. To her great relief he didn't comment on it, and she realised then that he saw nothing to be ashamed of in the human shape. He was not at all embarrassed—she was.

'I'll leave you to join me when you are ready,' he said, just as though he had discerned that there was no way she was going to get out of her dress with him standing there. Then before she could answer he had turned and headed for the water.

For a while Clare sat and watched, saw him start to swim out to sea with an easy powerful crawl. He had said he seldom bathed in the nude with women present, she recalled, as slowly she began to unbutton her dress. So at some time then he must have indulged in mixed bathing in the altogether. With the lack of shame he had for his own body that shouldn't have surprised her. What did surprise her was that when her thoughts went from there to the thought that he must have known the woman or women intimately to get to that state of affairs, she didn't find her thoughts at all pleasing.

She reached the water's edge, her eyes fixed on Lazar still swimming strongly. Slowly she waded in until the water was up to her waist, wishing mightily that she could swim with half the ease he had. That she couldn't swim had never bothered her before. In fact she couldn't ever remember having giving it any thought prior to coming here, but just then she would have given anything to have such glorious freedom of movement.

As she had two days previously, she enjoyed herself

splashing about, and was mildly astonished to discover she had lost some of her embarrassment at being so uncovered when Lazar swam up to her, his eyes flicking over her breasts just above the water as he stood up.

The sunlight glistened on the droplets of water on his shoulders and chest as with a careless hand he pushed his wet hair back. And then he was reaching out for her.

Beset with nerves, Clare was startled into the awareness of not being at all sure whether her nerves were because a very masculine male was about to touch her or if it was because she was about to have her first lesson in swimming.

'Lazar, I ... I've changed my mind,' she said, turning towards the beach, wanting to get there as quickly as her legs would take her.

Two hands came down on her shoulders, stopping her from going a step further. He must have felt the trembling that had taken her, for his voice was slightly shocked when he exclaimed:

'*Theos!* You are shaking!' Shock went from him, his voice changing to persuasive as he decided his own interpretation for her being so disturbed. 'There is nothing to be alarmed at, *pethi*,' and that teasing note again. 'Trust me, little Clare. I promise I will not drop you.'

She was sure it was just the desire to know the freedom he had shown in the water and nothing to do with the charm of the man himself, when, his voice coaxing, she just couldn't resist as he asked:

'Wouldn't you like to be able to swim?'

'Yes. Oh yes,' she said huskily. And that was all he waited to hear.

Without haste he turned her to face him. He looked

steadily into her eyes, then teased, 'Be brave, child. I have never drowned a pupil yet!'

Her nerves at the thought of having a man's arms around her bolted away at a different sort of panic— that of finding herself seemingly lying face down in the water as Lazar took her feet from under her. Instinctively she made a grab for him, only to hear his calm voice, telling her, 'Relax, Clare,' and repeating, 'I won't drop you.' Then she forgot everything save her confidence in him, and that regardless of elegance she was enjoying the feeling of being able to kick her legs out behind her.

Lazar gave her concise instructions which she followed as strictly as she could, concentrating with all her attention to get it right so that she forgot completely that his hands were touching any part of her. She was enjoying her lesson so much, it seemed to have lasted only two minutes when his voice somewhere above her head said:

'I think that is about enough for today.'

Disappointed, for they had only just started, she made a sudden movement of protest, caught him unawares, and for the briefest of moments her head went under.

Brief though it was before Lazar lifted her to stand up against him, she had taken fright. He was laughing at her, she knew, as he told her she had brought that on herself, but she couldn't have cared less about being laughed at as she gulped in fresh air.

Then suddenly he was no longer laughing. She felt the arm at her back tighten. She had up to that point been unaware that in her fright she had pressed up close to him, that her breasts were a soft cushion against his chest or that her thighs had pressed the water from against the front of his thighs so that the only contact was their skin.

But with his arm tightening at her back she did become aware of all these things, knew he too was aware of her body pressed close up to his, and with a horror that had her staring at him dumb-stricken, she realised she had aroused in him a feeling of desire.

That thought blanked out all other thought and feeling. Her childish splashing about took on nauseating proportions and she pushed forcefully at his chest with her hands.

He let her go at once, ready to wade back to where she had left her dress and hat. Striving for calm, Clare wondered if she had been crazy to imagine having her against him like that had stirred him to desire. For his voice didn't show that kind of emotion when he spoke, sounding perfectly controlled and in no way affected at having held her so close, as he casually remarked:

'You did quite well for your first lesson.' His voice was so totally normal she thought she just had to have imagined what she thought had gone on a moment ago. Surely a man couldn't change from desire to the mundane so easily? 'I told you I wouldn't drop you,' he added as they waded now only ankle-deep from the sea. 'You should have more faith in me, Clare.'

She reached the place where she had left her dress, now only partly in the shade, and stretched out a hand, only to have his voice staying her.

'Let the sun dry you first,' he suggested, evidently reading her intention to put her dress on over the top of her wet swimsuit.

She hesitated, saw Lazar was taking no more mind to her as he stretched out on the warm sand, closing his

eyes, apparently completely uncaring whether she followed his suggestion or not.

It would be just as easy to go back to the villa carrying her dress, she thought. It would only take a minute
or two to walk back. And yet she had spent too many
hours in the solitary confines of her room and she
didn't know that she wanted to go back yet.

Without her being aware of it her decision was made.
Her dress stayed where it was on the sand, a few
seconds later she was beside it. Sitting stiffly upright,
she flicked a glance at Lazar, a faint flickering of his
black lashes telling her he was not asleep but just taking this opportunity to relax and soak up the sun. His
features were even, looking chiselled in repose. Clare's
glance went to his mouth, then hurriedly she turned her
head, her eyes staring unseeing out to sea.

Some time before tomorrow she was supposed to go
and offer herself to him! Oh, how could she do it? But
if she didn't, what was to become of poor Kit? Lazar
had meant every word he had said—she had tried once
to get through to him and failed—and she just knew
she would be wasting her time trying again. She would
only make him angry with her.

Agitation tried to get the better of her at the thought
of how much more unbearable it would be if when she
went to him he took her in anger. No, no, she shied
from the thought. Don't let it be in anger.

Quite when she realised she was going to have to see
this thing through, that for Kit's sake she was going to
have to be very brave, she didn't know. But suddenly,
perhaps only five minutes later, she found she was
accepting the inevitability of what must happen.

Pictures of Kit, maybe wheelchair-bound for the rest

of his life, flashed through her mind, only for her to force them away as she tried to concentrate only on how kind Lazar had been with her yesterday. Perhaps it wouldn't be so bad. And anyway, wasn't she beginning to grow a little weary of the cowardly creature she was?

Her heartbeats quickening, she turned again to look at Lazar. His eyes were still closed. He looked to be completely oblivious to her sitting there beside him, yet she knew he must be aware she had not returned to the villa.

Once again she looked at his mouth, felt herself hypnotised by the warm curve of it. And then she knew for all her brave thoughts, for all her mental stiffening of her backbone, it would be absolutely impossible for her to tap on that communicating door tonight, to go to him cold, and announce, 'Here I am.'

She felt her stomach turn over at the thought, and had to grit her teeth to stay where she was, not to get up and bolt there and then.

It was daylight now, she forced herself to think rationally. If she had to take that gigantic plunge into womanhood, then wouldn't she feel better if she broke down some of the icy fear in her by experimenting while it was still light? Discovered what a kiss was like when there were no night-time gremlins to haunt her? Supposing it was horrible? Supposing in the dark that first kiss was vile? Supposing Lazar got furious with her if she fought that suffocating darkness of his kiss and for all he had said, it did turn out to be rape?

Realising she was on the verge of panicking, Clare grabbed at all the courage she could muster. It had to be now before that panic swamped her.

'Lazar,' she said quickly, and took fright when his

eyes opened and he looked straight into her own. Silently she battled not to run, swallowed hard, then said, 'Lazar, will you—k-kiss me?'

Idly he surveyed her flushed face, then to her utter mortification, 'No,' he replied succinctly. And not waiting to see what effect that had on her, he promptly closed his eyes again.

Completely shattered, she just sat and stared at him, her uppermost feeling one of mortification. He had no idea what it had cost her to make such a request, but to turn her down—just like that! Her feeling of mortification changed to one of absolute fury. She felt so violently angry she could have pummelled his head, that after she had dragged up every ounce of courage she possessed, he had coolly said 'No' and looked ready to go to sleep.

It was temper this time that would have had her storming back to the villa. But she was finding she was made of sterner material than she had thought. She just wouldn't go to his room cold tonight. She couldn't and wouldn't. It was too unthinkable that she should enter his room having had not even the merest contact with him of that sort, to have him douse the light and ...

'Why won't you kiss me?' she asked a minute or so later, her fury squashed under the weight of her having to force the issue. 'I thought that was what you w-wanted?'

This time he answered without bothering to open his eyes. 'If I remember rightly,' he corrected her lazily, 'the release of your brother depends on *you* kissing me.'

A small, 'Oh,' escaped her, and her temper surged into life again.

Angrily she looked at his still face and then to his

mouth. And as she looked, her temper, her anger left her. Something, she had no idea what, was urging her on to feel that mouth against hers. Confused, she turned her eyes seawards, staring at the horizon for long minutes until some compulsion so strong she couldn't ignore it had her turning back to look at him. His lashes were still now and frustratingly she thought he had nodded off.

Quietly, just in case, she asked, 'Are you asleep?'

Not a muscle flickered in his face to show he had heard, and then he was replying, 'No, I'm not asleep.' He didn't bother to open his eyes as he added, 'I'm here, ready and waiting to be—seduced.'

Shocked colour flooded her face, though for the briefest instant she thought a muscle had twitched near his mouth as though he was having a hard time not to laugh. That muscle stayed firm as she stared at it, but it didn't help the tumult of her emotions at all to suspect he might inwardly be laughing at her.

'I've never kissed anybody before,' came blurting out before she could stop it.

That had Lazar's eyes coming wide awake, showing the surprise with which he received her statement. Then his look hardened, an expression crossing his face which could only be translated as the Greek equivalent of 'Tell that to the Marines.' He closed his eyes again.

The minutes ticked by as Clare sat staring at him, her emotions growing to fever pitch as she realised if there was any kissing to be done, it was going to be up to her to do it.

Her face flushed, she edged nearer to him, the sun warm on her back, her body casting a shadow as gradually, very gradually she bent over him. Her face was very close to his, her heart pounding as though it would leap out of her body, when he made her aware he knew exactly what she was up to.

'Go on,' he urged, his eyes closed still, 'be a devil.'

Of course that had her backing away. But it was instinctive, and only for a few seconds. Then she brought her face close to his, and snatching at a wave of courage, she quickly touched her mouth to his, and just as quickly pulled back again—only to find she had no need at all to panic because there was not an atom of response coming from Lazar.

She turned her head seaward again, analysing to her surprise that not only had she liked that brief contact, but, shatteringly, had felt piqued that there had been no reaction from him.

Again she felt that same compulsion to look at him, not knowing who she was more annoyed with, herself or him that, by the look of it, he would shortly be asleep. She no longer had to force herself to experiment with the feel of his mouth beneath her own, and this time as she bent over and placed her dry lips over his she allowed her mouth to stay against his for a moment longer. Then she drew away hurriedly as she saw his eyes were open and those dark eyes were looking straight into hers. Trembling, she sat up straight. She had lost her voice, but she found that Lazar was having no such trouble.

'Is that the best you can do?' he queried softly, and never had she felt more totally inadequate.

'I told you,' she said stiffly, 'I don't know how.' Then her temper, her frustration and feelings of inadequacy all jumbled up together, and she exploded, 'It's like kissing a—a log!'

She watched his eyes narrow slightly, heard a small laugh escape him. 'Why not try it again?' he suggested softly, his voice encouraging.

Clare stared at him. She could feel a sort of fascination creeping over her, and yet she was wary. She had a feeling she was no longer the one in control of this kissing business.

'You won't ...' she began, the remembrance of how she had fainted that day he had held her in her mind, '... won't ...'

'I promise I won't do anything you won't want me to,' Lazar told her easily, lying perfectly still, his arms down by his sides.

Somewhere, somewhere in her head, warning bells were starting to go off, but for the first time in her life Clare took no notice of them. She had the greatest urge to feel Lazar's mouth again.

It felt exactly the same as the other two kisses, she thought, feeling strangely disappointed. But, just as she was about to remove her mouth from his, she felt his lips move, and a tingle of she knew not what shot through her. Startled, she made to jerk away, only to find Lazar had moved a hand to the back of her head and was holding her steady.

His mouth only inches from her own, he looked into her eyes. 'It's all right,' he soothed, just as though he was gentling a shying pony, 'all right,' he breathed softly, and she felt the gentle pressure of his hand bringing her head down again until her mouth met his.

With only the minutest of movement with his mouth, he had Clare discovering she was enjoying being kissed. He was in no hurry to force her through this first enormous barrier, and slowly, unaware of it, she relaxed. Again unhurriedly, he moved her until she was lying down too, the top half of her resting unashamedly over his chest.

He lifted her face to break his kiss, saw for himself there was no fear in her face, then brought her head down again, his mouth moving tantalisingly beneath her own, so that she had the feeling of wanting to move her mouth too.

Then Clare became aware of other movement as, not hurrying, he turned with her until it was she who was lying on her back, she with Lazar's chest over hers— and it was Lazar who was doing the kissing.

With her arms down by her sides, Lazar's arms one either side of her, not touching, she wondered what she had been afraid of. This mutual kissing between a man and a woman was really very pleasurable. Somehow her eyes had instinctively closed, but she opened them again, innocently enchanted, when Lazar pulled his head up to gaze deeply into her brown pools of openness.

'*Theos!*' he breathed on a hushed note, her innocence there for all the world to see. 'I didn't believe you, but you really haven't been kissed before, have you?'

'I—I think I like it,' she said, not recognising that husky voice as her own.

And Lazar smiled, his shaken look changing to one of teasing as he asked softly, 'Only think?'

Her face pink, the husky stranger inside her answered, 'No—I kn-know I like it.'

He laughed at her reply, a gentle laugh as though her answer had pleased him, seeming to have forgotten which one of them was supposed to do the seducing, for Clare felt seduced by the way his lightened look took those years away from him. She found herself asking:

'W-would you do it again, please?'

For a moment she thought she had been too forward, for the light look left him as he stared sternly at her. Was he considering her question seriously she wondered, or ... His hand came to her face, a gentle finger running over her lips, his touch making her tingle again, before he used that finger to part her lips.

'Keep your mouth like that the next time I kiss you,' he instructed, his hand moving away.

'Like this?' she mumbled, and left her lips parted.

Lazar lowered his head and as his mouth claimed hers, Clare, with a veritable explosion of feelings inside her, knew that this was what kissing really was. The other kisses he had given her were just a preliminary to the real thing. His lips were parted as he had instructed hers to be. His mouth was mobile, seeking, receiving, making her mouth mobile too without her even having to think about it.

She tensed in momentary shock when she felt his tongue tip on the inside of her bottom lip, and her hands came up to grip hard on to his naked shoulders. Her heart pounding madly, she pulled away.

'Are you all right?' Lazar asked, nothing urgent in his tone.

Chokily, she answered, 'Yes,' knowing herself uncertain.

Something was going on in her nether regions of which she had no experience. She felt on shaking ground, unsure, her only certainty being she wanted him to kiss her again. The hands holding tensely on to his shoulders suddenly relaxed. Of their own volition her lips parted the way he had instructed this time by instinct—in invitation. A small light of triumph appeared in his eyes as he gazed at her sweet supplication, then Lazar was claiming her mouth, his hands coming up to caress her shoulders, in delicious, tingling movements.

Thinking was a thing of the past as Clare gave herself up to this newly discovered world of kisses, her body feeling she would be ready to stay there all day enjoying this wonderful intimacy.

His mouth left hers to plant tiny kisses on her throat, she heard a low moan escape him, and was in heaven because she too felt like moaning with the pleasure of it all. She was in the seventh heaven of delight while his hand continued to caress her shoulders, and gave her lips readily when once more he took them.

And then, shockingly, something else was happening. While the very heat of her blood turned to fire, Lazar's one hand left her shoulder and with consummate ease caressed its way across her breastbone and beneath the top of her swimsuit, not stopping until it had captured the swollen rise of her breast, naked beneath his hand.

The feel of his hand, his fingers caressing tenderly over the hardened peak, was so personal, so unexpected, she couldn't believe it was happening. Shocked out of the feeling of mutual gratification, a strangled gasp broke from her. From somewhere three times her normal strength had her pushing him violently away, then she was on her feet, her eyes wide and horrified.

'Oh!' she cried hoarsely, her sudden scarlet colour changing to ashen.

Lazar was on his feet too witnessing her distress, her horror. His hands stretched towards her as he took a step nearer.

'Do not be afraid,' he said quietly, 'I ...'

'You ... You ...' She was struggling for words, back-

ing away, her face bereft of colour as new knowledge
of herself took hold. 'You ...' came strangled from her
again, her eyes huge in her blood-drained face, this new
unbelievable truth threatening to have her collapsing.

'Oh God!' she groaned, and as Lazar went to take
another step forward, she turned and fairly flew across
the sand.

CHAPTER SIX

CLARE was shaking uncontrollably when she reached
her room, her breath harsh and panting. She gripped
hard on to the end of the bed as the shock of what
had happened slowly receded—but not the shock of
her discovery. Who was this new person who had
awakened within her in the hot summer climes of
Northern Greece?

She had been aware of a growing dissatisfaction with
the person she was before she had left England, but
within the space of less than a week, new life had
surged up from the depths of her being. Temper she
had never before possessed had spurted to the surface
on at least two occasions she could recall. Violent anger
too, that had her wanting to hit a man without the
semi-hysteria that had been there that time she had hit
him.

And now this other shattering new emotion she had
discovered out there on the beach. This person within
her enjoyed being kissed—had kissed back with heat
that had come naturally from her—and, oh God, that
wanton female had come to life and had so shaken her
she had had to run. For feeling rocked to her very

foundations to find Lazar's hand on that very private part of her, she had discovered that far from not wanting his hand touching her breast, he had aroused in her a desire to have his hand there, and not just that, but more, much more.

Had that really been her out there? She who ever since that night five years ago had been protected with a zeal that would put many a uniformed guard to shame.

Wishing she could stop shaking, Clare groped to sit on the bed, her legs unable to support her any longer. She was confused now as to whether or not Lazar had desired her, was too shattered to get her thoughts straight about what effect she had had on him. She knew only in her bewildered state that whether he wanted her or not—God help her, nothing had prepared her that *she* should want him.

Trying to get herself under control but feeling an ache for his touch, she was nowhere near to getting on top as she recalled that new wonderful excitement he had brought to life within her, when her bedroom door opened and sent all thoughts flying.

Her head jerked up, her face still a shocked white, to see Lazar standing there. Her hat, dress and sandals in his hands told her he had picked them up when he had followed her from the beach. He stood making no attempt to come into the room, his expression stern as he surveyed the way she couldn't stop shaking, the paleness of her, her eyes over-large in her face.

'You need a drink.' His voice sounded like gravel in her ears, and she could have wept that to him she must seem like an immature schoolgirl. 'We both do,' he added shortly, then tossed her things to the bed. 'Get dressed, then join me in the *salóni*.'

Not anywhere near ready to have any sort of conversation with him, Clare felt too vulnerable to have him return to her room with the drink he said she needed. She didn't want him coming back and finding her still in her swimsuit.

Hoping that if she was fully dressed some of her scattered wits might return, she went to the bathroom, quickly showering grains of sand from her body. When she was dressed she found that though her shaking had lessened, she still felt too mixed up to face Lazar.

But she had to go. She didn't want him here in the intimacy of her bedroom. She wasn't yet at home with this new passionate being she had discovered inside her; she was wary of her, didn't trust her.

Lazar was standing staring out of the window when Clare nervously entered the *salóni*. He had a glass of something in his hand and by the damp look of his hair he too had taken a quick shower before changing into a fresh shirt and trousers.

As quietly as she had come in, he had heard her. He turned, his eyes going over her still pale face. He looked as stern as he had in her room, she thought, her insides fluttering. But suddenly his sternness left him—and she wished it hadn't, for he gave her a gentle smile that threatened to have her insides breaking up.

'How are you feeling now?' he asked quietly.

'F-fine,' she stammered, and wasn't allowed to feel awkward a moment longer when he indicated the couch.

'Sit there. I'll fix you a drink.'

She smelt brandy in the glass he handed her, but didn't want it so made no attempt to sip at it. But she had reckoned without Lazar standing over her and instructing kindly:

'Drink it down, Clare. You will feel better for it.'

Perhaps he discerned that to have him so close, so tall above her was unnerving her further, because without waiting to see whether she was obeying him, he strolled back to his position by the window.

Clare took a sip of the brandy, felt the fire of the liquid as it went down. Then knowing it was sacrilege and would have her father who fancied he knew a good brandy frowning in horror, she gulped the rest down in one go. If Lazar said she would feel better for drinking it she was prepared to believe him. It was worth trying anything if it would make her feel better than she did right now.

She set the glass down on a low table nearby, the small sound it made causing Lazar to look her way. An expression of satisfaction crossed his features to see the glass empty, but when she would have got to her feet and disappeared back to her room his voice stopped her.

'Don't go, Clare,' he said, and for all his voice was quiet, she sensed an order behind his words.

'I—th-thought you ... I only came for—b-because you said I should have a drink,' she said, standing up.

'Sit down,' he commanded, coming up close, but making no attempt to push her down to her seat or in any way touch her.

The brandy was warming her insides, and quite suddenly her world didn't seem anywhere near as topsy-turvy as it had. She sat down without further protest. Only to have her nerves jumping again when Lazar elected to occupy part of the same couch. Her nerves quietened when she observed there was room enough for a third person to take a seat in between them, and that Lazar was making no effort to close the gap.

For countless seconds silence reigned, and for the life of her she couldn't be the one to break it. Lazar was studying the glass in his hand as though it held the key to anything he might have to say to her, giving her the oddest impression that he was choosing his words very carefully.

She flinched when he moved, the suddenness of his movement as he bent to place his glass on the table next to hers telling her he had decided on what he was going to say.

Fully expecting him to tear her apart for leading him on by asking him to kiss her—she blushed at the memory—and then running away, she received yet another shock that however hard he had tried to dress it up, his words came out bluntly, and tore at her shredded nerve ends.

'Tell me, Clare,' he said, his voice not unkind. 'Why is it that you are so afraid of men?'

Her gasp was audible, though little else left her throat as she stared at him in horror. 'I ...' she managed to choke, but couldn't carry on.

'Do not be alarmed,' he gentled her. 'I'm not going to harm you, but ...' he paused, then looking straight into her eyes he added softly, 'But it is important to me that I should know.'

'I ...' she began again, nothing coming through from her grey matter to tell her why it should be so important to him. 'I'm not afraid ...' was as far as she managed, getting more confused as the thought visited her that she wasn't afraid of men any longer—well, not of Lazar, not in a physical context anyway.

'Oh, Clare,' he sighed, regretfully, she thought, that she should lie to him, 'I have witnessed too many things about you for that to be true. I apologise now for being too late with my conclusions and subjecting you to more than you could handle out there.'

Her nerves settled as curiosity stirred, for all her face went pink at his reminder of the intimacies that had taken place on the beach. What was it he had witnessed prior to her bolting just now that had him taking this line of thinking? She had up until a couple of hours ago been no different, she thought, from the way she had always been; less afraid if anything, she mused, remembering her happy day yesterday.

'I don't know why you should think—th-that about me,' she said bravely, wondering how much courage came from her and how much from the generous brandy she had downed. 'But ...'

'Clare, Clare,' he shushed her. 'Everything points to it, only I have been too occupied with other thoughts to see it.' Incapable of replying, she stared at him and he continued, 'I have eyes in my head, have seen the way you attempt to hide your—femininity in shapeless garments, seen the way you tremble whenever the subject of your coming to my room has been mentioned. I have had you faint in my arms when you thought I was going to kiss you, have seen you run away terrified when that kiss happened and I let that kiss take its natural course.'

Her cheeks bright crimson, wishing he would get off the subject, Clare realised it would be the utmost folly at this juncture to reveal that it had been that 'natural course' that had her running away, but not because his touch had been loathsome. She studied the pattern of her dress covering her knees, her throat locked, and Lazar went on persuasively.

'You were in shock when I came to bring your clothes,' he said, still talking to her in a low gentle voice. 'I think maybe you still are a little, though the brandy has helped your colour. But I think for your own good, little Clare, we have to talk this out.'

'Lazar, I . . .' Clare found her voice. If he was going to start dissecting what had happened down on the beach she knew she just wasn't going to be able to take it. 'Please, Lazar, I don't want to talk about it.'

'We have to, Clare,' he said, his voice taking on an uncompromising note as again he told her, 'It is important to me—to both of us.'

She tried to think why it was so important, then suddenly realised why. Lazar's family code of honour demanded that he took from her what her brother was said to have taken from Sophronia, and he had been ready to carry out without mercy the intent of his threat. Had she not seen a different side to him yesterday she would have said he was still ready to carry out that threat. Yet he had been a pleasing companion yesterday; considerate to her welfare—he needn't have bought her that sun hat, needn't have taken her out at all, for that matter, either. But he had. And that spoke of something in him, a sensitivity perhaps. A sensitivity that now said as great as his family honour was, if it was true that she was afraid of men—if there was good cause for her fear—then maybe he would not be able to bring himself to carry out that revenge. Hope surged within her. Her natural reserve having returned, the passionate-natured girl she had discovered on the beach relegated to her proper place.

'Lazar . . .' she said, her voice quick, her mood anxious, wanting to tell him now what she had thought would never be dragged from her to tell anybody. But the words were sticking in her throat and wouldn't come. They had been walled up inside her for too long.

And it was then, as though he could see she was on the brink of telling him what he wanted to know, as though he knew the struggle she was having to get the words out, that Lazar narrowed the gap between them. He moved to sit close to her, to encourage her, his hands taking hers in a warm loose hold.

'Why is it, Clare,' he asked very softly, 'that you, an Englishwoman, have passed your nineteenth birthday and had not until this afternoon received your first kiss?'

Her face working, seeing yet not seeing the gentle understanding in him, she struggled to release the words. He waited patiently, not hurrying her.

And suddenly, like the deadly dark secret she felt it to be, it wouldn't stay buried any longer. As if held down these last five years by a tightly coiled spring held fast by a very stout unbreakable lock, that lock broke, the spring was released, and one sentence came rocketing into the air, sounding loud and discordant as it bounced round the room and came back to reverberate deafeningly in her ears.

'I was attacked when I was fourteen,' she said, and it was too late to try and dress it up when she saw and heard his shocked reaction.

An explosive stream of Greek shot from him, giving her an impression that even if she did know the language then that string of invective would not be found in any Greek dictionary. Then all she was aware of was a numbing pain in her hands as Lazar's grip tightened, threatening to fracture every bone.

He gained control after a moment, and the bruising

intensity of his hold lessened, his voice calm, when he requested:

'Tell me about it, Clare.'

Horrified at the idea, she shook her head, then found he was locking her eyes to his, hypnotising her with some need he had to know everything. 'I can't!' she cried, knowing nothing would have her dredging all that up from the dark corners of her mind.

'Please,' he said, just the one word.

'I can't!' she cried again, but found his eyes on hers were having a mesmeric effect on her. 'I . . .' she tried to protest once more, but the 'can't' wouldn't come.

With his eyes holding hers she found she could not deny him—could deny him nothing. She shook her head hopelessly. Lazar had said nothing since that quietly spoken 'Please', his very silence causing a weakening inside her she thought had very little to do with the brandy she had drunk. Tearing her eyes away from his pinning gaze, she felt words coming to the surface, her unconscious vow of silence fracturing.

Her eyes fixed on the wall opposite, the words started to leave her. 'We live in a fairly isolated village,' she began, forgetful that he had been there. She cleared her choked throat. 'It's a rural community and because we don't have a library the mobile library van calls every two weeks. Nobody wanted to go that particular Monday, but because my mother had a book out that everybody was queueing up to read I said I would take it back for her.'

She hesitated, seeing everything with horrible clarity in her mind, and frightened to look further. She glanced back at Lazar, wanting to ask him not to make her say more. The look on his face was kind, gentle, understanding, and she thought he was going to let her leave it there.

'Go on, Clare,' he said steadily, his hold on her hands firming.

Her glance left him, returning to the wall. 'There was a queue at the van, there always was, but I didn't mind. There were a couple of girls I knew on the same errand and we got chatting so that the hour the van stayed was nearly up by the time we giggled our way into the van.'

She was quite unaware of the fact she had just revealed that up until then she had been a perfectly normal schoolgirl.

'I knew I was going to be later getting home than my family would have thought, but I wasn't too bothered because I'd managed to get another book I knew would please my mother.' Her voice began to falter. 'Th-there's a dark lane j-just before you come to our house——' She stopped, a sickness starting up inside. 'I—I was nearly to the t-top of—of it ...' Her voice petered out, her hands gripping Lazar's fiercely now, though she was entirely unaware of it.

'You were nearly to the top of the lane,' prompted a disembodied voice by her side.

'It was pitch bl-black—I'd forgotten to take a torch. Someone said "Hello"—a m-man. "Hello", I called back.' Her fingers were mutilating the hands holding hers, but no sound came from Lazar. Seconds passed, then that voice prompted quietly:

'So you called back a greeting.'

'And the next thing I knew——' Her voice rose, her agitation had her hands leaving his, going to his arms, to his shirt sleeves, her stare coming away from the wall

as a feeling of dizziness came over her. She fought her
way out of it, some inner self telling her she had to
finish it. 'I was being punched, beaten,' a separate part
of her registered that Lazar's colour had gone, her voice
rising higher she saw his face whiten, 'thrown ...' she
said, gulping for air as she came to the end, 'thrown to
the ground.'

Near to fainting, having spoken her nightmare as
she relived the experience, she clutched at the man beside her, seeing only greyness. She came to her full self
to find she was lying on the couch with Lazar stooped
on the floor beside her stroking the hair back from her
forehead with a gentle hand.

'So that is why your brother was screaming abuse
down the phone to me. Why Aeneas is having such a
hard time with him,' Lazar said absently, there being
just one more question he wanted the answer to.

Clare felt weak, as though the stuffing had been taken
out of her. She must get to her room, she thought. She
wanted to be by herself. She was only half aware that
she had told Lazar everything, yet knowing she must
have done. Though she couldn't understand why he
was looking at her as though he had more he wanted to
know—how could there be? He had stripped her bare
of all there was to know!

'Clare.' His hand left her forehead to take hold of
hers, to grip them tightly when he saw she was looking at him wanting to know what that 'Clare' had been
about. 'Did he rape you, *pethi*?'

Somehow she seemed to know that *pethi* was Greek
for child, maybe because he had called her that once
before, just before he had instructed her in the water
to 'Be brave, child.' Perhaps she did seem like a child
to him, she thought tiredly, then as the grip on her

hands tightened the longer he waited for her answer, she shook her head and told him wearily:

'No.' Some of the force went out of those fingers. 'B-because I was late home my father came to look for me. He must have heard me screaming before he turned the lane, because suddenly I couldn't scream at all. I remember I tried all I could to scream when I saw the searching light from his torch, but no sound would come. And then my father w-was pulling the man away from me. I was free and ... and my father was half killing him.'

'Only half killing him!' The gentle air which had been with Lazar ever since she had got started evaporated, leaving her in no doubt that he would have done a full job of it. 'He was prosecuted—this *nothos*?'

Nothos was probably right whatever it meant, Clare thought dully. 'No,' she replied, a shuddering breath leaving her. 'I w-was ill for a time. My Aunt Katy is a doctor, so she looked after me. My parents decided not to call in the police because they were afraid it would retard my recovery. B-besides, I wouldn't have been able to give evidence anyway.'

'You were so long in shock!'

'I couldn't speak for over twelve months. It was awful,' she understated.

Lazar looked as though he was going to take her in his arms to comfort her—she saw his arms move. But he checked their movement, not knowing that she no longer had any fear of being in his arms.

'So this—this apology for a man got away with only a hiding from your father he wouldn't forget?'

'Yes,' she whispered. 'I overheard my parents talking and knew they were worried in case he did the same again to another girl. He was a man who worked on one of the farms, so we all knew who he was. And then about a year later I read in the local paper that he had over-turned a tractor and had been killed. My voice started to come back then.'

Feeling drained, absolutely nothing more she could tell him, Clare moved to sit up. 'I'd like to go to my room now, Lazar,' she said, sounding as exhausted as she looked. He would have to move to allow her to get by. Her legs felt too weak to have her scrambling to the other end of the couch.

He smiled, a smile that was compassionate and warmed her heart. 'Yes,' he agreed, 'I think it will be as well for you to rest until it is time for dinner.'

Standing up, he allowed her the space she needed. Getting to her feet, her legs wobbly, Clare would have stumbled, but Lazar was there holding her steady. Then giving her a look that was at once reassuring, he picked her up in his arms, commenting in case she hadn't read his look:

'You have nothing to fear from me, Clare. I just think you will get to your room more quickly if I carry you there.'

Impersonally he took her to her room, gently set-ting her down on the bed, taking off her sandals and pulling a light cover up around her.

'Rest now, *pethi*,' he said softly, and left her.

Sleep was a million miles away when he had gone. But as she lay there strength gradually returned to her limbs and her mind slowly cleared of the remem-brance of that terrible ordeal.

Her thoughts drifted on to how gentle Lazar had been with her, and recalling the way he had been she could not regret she had told him what she had, even though part of her mind registered astonishment that she had done so.

Not understanding quite how Lazar had changed in her thoughts from devil to near saint, Clare got up from the bed and found momentary respite from her thoughts in going to the bathroom and shampooing the sea water from her hair. She towelled it vigorously, but found as she brushed the air through her long tresses in order for it to dry so she should appear looking respectable at dinner, that there was no easy way to get Lazar out of her mind.

In the middle of pleasant thoughts about him, of how, now that he knew about her, she was fairly certain he would not keep her to the price he had said she must pay if Kit was to be saved, she woke up with a start to the thought that it had been ages since she had given Kit any thought.

Dear God, what had happened to her in this beautiful part of the world? How could she have pushed the danger Kit was in so easily to the back of her mind? What had happened to her that not only should she have put her worries for her brother to one side but that here in these lovely surroundings so many of her indelibly held beliefs about herself should have been stood on their heads and she should turn out not at all the sort of person she had thought herself to be?

How could she have forgotten about Kit? How could she have been so complimenting herself that she need not have to go to Lazar to offer herself—her brow puckered at the feeling that tripped her up that she wanted to feel that warm mobile mouth over hers again. She forced herself to concentrate on Kit, albeit belatedly. What had she been thinking of not to see that if she didn't go to Lazar, then that still left Kit to take the punishment she should have stood proxy for?

She checked her watch. There was another hour to go before dinner. She wanted to see Lazar straight away, wanted to know what was going to happen to Kit— to plead if necessary that he shouldn't harm him. And yet everything she had babbled out to him having come back to her, she experienced embarrassment at having to face him again. There was only an hour to wait, she told herself, shyness making her buck the issue. It would take her half that time to shower and dress.

Her hair looked pretty, she thought, when she stood surveying her image after completing her ablutions. On an impulse to look more grown up than the *pethi* Lazar had called her, she found the lipstick he had given her and lightly coloured her mouth.

The girl who looked back at her wasn't at all the girl who had stepped on to that plane—was it only Monday night? The faintest shade of tan was begin- ning to touch her skin, taking away that pale look that had deadened the vitality of her silvery tresses. Her mouth too seemed to have come alive. Was it just the lipstick that had done that? Or was it that being thoroughly kissed by Lazar had brought her lips to ripeness?

Blushing at her thoughts, dragging her mind away from the wonder of those kisses, Clare could no longer stand looking at herself. She sat in one of the two chairs in her room to wait until it was time to join Lazar for dinner. She must forget about herself, of how, only now she was beginning to face, Lazar Var- dakas had brought a dormant Clare Harper to life. She must concentrate all her thoughts on Kit. Lazar must be made to see that he couldn't carry out his intention that Kit should be physically assaulted.

With a fast beating heart she realised the time had come when she had to face Lazar. She found herself accepting the new thinking Clare who, as she got up from the bed, wished she had something better to wear to grace his table than what she had on. His description of 'bell tent' was very apt, she thought, as she left her room.

She saw Lazar as she turned into the hall. He looked tall and magnificent, she couldn't help thinking, as he stood by the dining room door waiting for her so she should enter in front of him. He was wearing dark trousers and another of his fine, polo-necked black body shirts that showed the strength of his muscles.

Aware of his scrutiny as she approached, she saw his eyes linger on her cloud of newly washed hair. Then she was up to him, a shy smile on her mouth. She thought perhaps he might ask her how she was or possibly say something to ease the situation if he guessed this was an awkward moment for her. But her smile faded into nothing as she saw his eyes on her mouth, saw his lips firm as his eyes met hers—and then found herself on the receiving end of the coldest look she had so far received from him.

Rooted, she stared at him. What was wrong? Where was the kind considerate man who not too many hours before had carried her to lay her gently down on her bed?

'Lazar, what ...?' she began, only to feel a fool to have said anything, when over the top of her he said coolly: 'After you,' letting her know he was more interested in having his dinner than in having a conversation with her in the hall, and since she was now blocking the doorway, she was holding up the proceedings.

Clare felt herself freezing up inside. Her expression solemn, she turned and walked into the dining room, taking her by now usual place at the table. What had happened to him? she wondered in bewilderment, any questions she had to ask him about Kit pushed out of her mind by her confusion at this hard-eyed stranger sitting opposite.

Rasmus came in, unobtrusively serving a meal that though deliciously cooked tasted like nothing in her mouth. Silently the meal continued. What Lazar was thinking Clare had no idea, but he was making no attempt to converse as he had on other occasions, and back in her shell, she found she just couldn't bring herself to break the oppressive air in the room.

Swallowing became difficult, her nerves stretching to breaking point so that when her dessert arrived, it was no surprise to her that she lost her grip on her spoon and it went spinning from her hand. A blush coloured her cheeks as she bent to pick it up, only to halt half way as Lazar rapped out curtly, 'Leave it.'

Rasmus finished serving his master the cheese and biscuits he preferred and smiling at Clare placed a fresh spoon on the table in front of her. Wanting to push the dish of fresh fruit salad and ice cream away, wanting to race from the table and shut herself in her room, Clare forced herself to stay. She had to ask about Kit if it killed her. She waited only until Rasmus had left the room with their used dishes, then struggled to find her voice.

'Lazar,' she began, feeling that with him in this mood he would probably prefer it if she called him Mr

Vardakas, 'Lazar, I—there's something I wanted to ask ...'

To her amazement he stood up, not allowing her to finish. 'I'm afraid whatever it is will have to wait,' she was told coldly. 'I have to be at the hospital shortly.'

'Oh.' He was at the door before her mind caught up with what he had said, then a semi-relief surged through her. It wasn't her he was so out of sorts with! He must be terribly worried about his uncle. At the door he half turned and her sympathetic smile winged to him. 'Oh, Lazar, I'm so sorry. Is your uncle worse?'

If it was possible his face hardened further at her smile, his glance flicking her face. She saw a muscle move in his jaw. 'No,' he said distinctly. 'He is improving by the hour.'

Had he slapped her Clare could not have felt more wounded. But he was not waiting to see how she took his departing remark, the door closed after him and she was alone.

Her glance returned to the table, to where he had sat, his biscuits and cheese untouched. He can't bear to be in my company! She couldn't stop the thought. Then like a bolt from the blue another thought flashed into her mind, and she saw then what her naïve mind had not been able to pick up all through the meal.

She had disgusted him with her revelations, disgusted him so much she had turned his stomach. He had eaten barely anything either, she recalled, hadn't spoken to her because just the sight of her made him nauseous. He couldn't bear looking at her, hadn't even been able to stick it out and wait for his coffee.

Appalled that Lazar, who had been so kind to her in her distress, should when he had carried her out of

his sight—carried her, she saw now, in order to get
her out of the way more quickly—have then got round
to thinking that the blame for that terrible episode was
entirely hers, she could not stay staring at the chair he
had so recently occupied.

She was crying by the time she got to her room, hurt
to her very soul that she had told him everything. Revealed to him things he had insisted on knowing, things
that had been so tightly locked up within her she
couldn't even talk to her family about them. Was she
so wrong to have told him? But how could she have
done any other? He had looked determined to know.
Yet to have told him all, received his understanding—
she had been so sure of that understanding too—only
to have him think over what she had told him and end
up disgusted with her, made her deeply upset.

Perhaps Greek women were thought lower than low
when and if such a thing happened to them, she
thought, wishing she had found out more about their
culture before she had said anything. Lazar had said
Sophronia's chances of making a suitable marriage
were now nil because of what Kit was supposed to have
done. So perhaps being the innocent victim of an attack
carried the same sort of slur.

She could feel his disgust now like salt in a raw
wound, and didn't know why it should matter so much
that by revealing what she had she had earned his con-
tempt.

Rinsing her face, she decided she might as well go to
bed. A wry thought came as she reached for a towel.
Since he loathed her so much she was sure she had no
reason to worry about Lazar expecting her in his bed
tonight. He would turf her out on her ear if she so
much as rattled his door knob. But whether he liked

it or not she was going to have to tackle him in the
morning about Kit. Tomorrow was Saturday, the last
day of the time he had allotted her.

Clare lay awake for what seemed an age. At midnight she looked at her watch and quelled the feeling
that came with being thought the dregs; they certainly
kept some strange visiting hours at whatever hospital
Lazar's uncle was in. The idea came that he might
be with some woman—some sophisticated woman,
she amended. Some sophisticated, untarnished—untarnished? She doubted it—woman who wouldn't take
very long to make him forget the disgust he felt with
Clare Harper.

The thought that he was with a woman made her
feel sick, but she wasn't very surprised. Everything she
had thought about since she had come to bed had disturbed her. Emotionally worn out after everything that
had happened that day, she turned out the lamp and
moved to her side. Two minutes later she was raising
her head from her pillow listening to the purr of a
car that could be heard coming down the drive. Her
head fell back to her pillow and within minutes she
was fast asleep.

For the first few hours her sleep was satisfying. Then
she stirred and opened her eyes to find it was still dark.
Stretching out a hurried hand for her watch, she saw
from its illuminated dial that it was ten past three.
She hated the dark, wished it was daylight. Close your
eyes, try to get back to sleep again, she told herself.
When you open your eyes again it will be daylight.

She closed her eyes, thought of her family, thought
of Lazar in the room next door. She thought of Kit.
They were going to beat Kit if she couldn't stop them,
so she had to stop them. She had to stop them, they

couldn't beat Kit. She had been beaten once—she mustn't think about that. Think about your family. Think about Kit—Clare fell into an uneasy sleep.

They were going to beat Kit. They mustn't beat him, they mustn't beat him. They mustn't beat—*her*! It was dark in the lane. Who ... She was frightened. Who ... No! No, stop. Stop it. *Stop! Stop!* No!!! Somebody was screaming, screaming, dreadful terrified screams, horrendous screams. Why didn't they stop? Stop—*stop*! Oh God, that bloodcurdling scream. Why didn't they stop? She was frightened. Somebody was being tortured! Oh, please stop. Please, *please* stop. She couldn't bear it. What was happening? Why was that man ... Why couldn't she scream? Her mouth was open, forcing sound, but no sound was coming. He was going to hit her again....

CHAPTER SEVEN

'CLARE! Wake up, Clare!'

Someone shaking her, calling her name brought her out of her frightening nightmare. Bathed in sweat, she opened wild terror-filled eyes, as blinding light struck her.

'You are safe now, *agapémene*,' Lazar told her urgently. 'You are safe, Clare, nothing will harm you.'

Wide-eyed, she looked at him, having no idea how long he had been there trying to shake her awake, but feeling no surprise that he should be there and not her parents as her eyes took in that the communicating door between the two rooms was wide open as though her screams had brought him in jet-propelled.

Strong hands were holding her shoulders, to her distressed vision his face looked grey. She opened her mouth to tell him she was all right, but no sound came from her fear-dried throat.

'*Theos!*' Lazar exclaimed as he witnessed the difficulty she was having in endeavouring to form her words, and she thought he lost more colour. 'Speak to me, Clare,' he demanded, recovering. 'For the love of God say something—anything!'

Her mouth working, she tried for all she was worth, knowing fear that she might never speak again. The hands on her shoulders tightened their grip.

'Try Clare, try,' he urged, her fear communicating itself to him.

She sucked in dry breath, her eyes wild again, panic-filled. Then as she let her breath out a painful, harsh shuddering sound came with it.

'Oh—Lazar!' broke from her, and she began to sob.

'Thank God!' he breathed, and she was in his arms, being rocked like a baby, while over and over he said, '*Agapémene, agapémene.* You are safe now.'

His words comforted her, but the tears just wouldn't stop as she clutched on to him as though frightened he might go away, leaving her in the dark.

Minutes passed while he sat holding her sob-racked body. Then words came from her without thought. 'It wasn't—my fault,' she sobbed brokenly, her fingers convulsively clutching and unclutching the back of him. 'I couldn't h-help it.'

Lazar tried to shush her, his one arm round her waist, his other stroking her hair in soothing movements. But she didn't want to be shushed and became more agitated.

'It wasn't!' she cried. 'I'm not to blame.'

'What are you not to blame for, Clare?' he asked gently, sensing she had a worry that had to be talked out.

'I dis-disgusted you whe-when I told you—about me. You thought it w-was all my fault. But it wasn't—it wasn't,' she broke off to hiccup a sob. 'You were awful to me at dinner, but I couldn't help it. He—he grabbed m-me . . .'

A whole stream of Greek left Lazar as, still holding on to her, he pushed her away so he could see into her unhappy eyes. Clare caught the stunned look on his face and wondered if she had read his reason for being the way he had at dinner totally wrong.

'Clare, beautiful little Clare,' he said, reverting to English now that he had adjusted to what she had said, 'I wasn't disgusted—not with you. How could I be, my little innocent?'

'You weren't?' she said, her sobs dying as she stared at him wide-eyed.

'Not with you,' he repeated, admitting, 'I did feel disgust, yes, but only because your father had not done a full job of killing the man.'

'But—but at dinner . . .' she faltered on a shuddering breath as a dry sob shook her body.

'Forgive me, I was a brute,' Lazar apologised. 'What you told me upset me a little. I knew I had put you through hell in making you tell me—and this night-mare proves it. I was afraid of something like this happening. Having dragged all that out of you I wanted you to go to bed with a clear mind—I was afraid to say anything to you that might have you fear-ing me in the room next door. I purposely stayed out until I thought you would be asleep.'

He pulled her to him again, cradling her loosely in his arms, his hand moving to smooth the hair back from her brow as he had done the previous afternoon. Clare wanted to tell him she had no fear of him, not in the way he meant, but the words wouldn't come. Gently he continued to hold her, soothing her, until gradually the terror of her nightmare left her.

She had witnessed this gentleness in him before, knew he had a fine sensitivity, and suddenly she was forgetting her own need for comfort. It becoming urgent that Lazar should know some comfort too since he must be blaming himself that he had brought this on.

'Lazar,' she said softly, and the brief stilling of his hand on her forehead told her she had his attention. She pulled to sit up, and immediately he let her go. 'It wasn't you—my telling you—you know—that was responsible for my having a nightmare.' Perhaps that was a bit of a lie, but that wasn't important. 'I've been having nightmares for years,' and at his quick look, 'but not as frequently now as I used to.'

She had been no comfort at all, she could see that. She could see he was still blaming himself. And it came to her then that he was so set on taking all the blame that anything she might say was going to be disbelieved. Perhaps even the sight of her had him inwardly whipping up anger against himself.

'I'll be all right now,' she told him, knowing he would get her meaning that she was ready to be left on her own.

'Do you have a spare nightdress?' he asked, startling her by the unexpected question into pointing and answering:

'There's one in that bottom drawer, but ...'

'The one you are wearing is soaked through,' he told her, going over to the chest of drawers.

Only then did she become aware that she was sitting up in a cotton nightdress that clung damply after the sweat of fear had lathered her. For the first time too she became aware of the way in which Lazar was dressed. She had been too upset to notice before. But now as he extracted a nightdress from one of the drawers she saw he appeared to be wearing nothing but a hastily pulled on robe, his legs bare from below knee level reminding her vividly of the few clothes that had separated them when she had discovered she wanted more than just kisses from him.

Her face was stained crimson at her thoughts when he came back to the bed. She saw his face tighten momentarily as he observed her blush, saw his eyes flick to her well defined breasts, and held her breath as the most wanton of feelings rioted through her.

'It's all right, Clare.' The tight look left him. 'I do not intend to personally change your nightwear.'

He dropped the nightdress near her hand, then walked round to the other side of the bed to switch on the small bedside lamp.

'Get into your dry nightdress as soon as I've gone,' he instructed, then with a swift look at her, he strode to switch off the centre light and through the communicating door. Clare wanted to thank him for coming to her, but the door had closed.

For a while she lay just thinking about him, about that treacherous feeling she had had of wanting him to kiss her again. It was a joy to her to know she was normal, to know she hadn't been permanently damaged by what had happened five years ago, but for a moment she had cause to chew at her bottom lip, remembering she had felt quite wanton just before Lazar had left, and wondering if it had sent her to the other extreme. But the thought didn't stay, because it wasn't every man she felt that way about. Though she couldn't figure out just why it was only Lazar Vardakas who stirred her in that particular fashion.

She was still awake when the first fingers of dawn crept across the night sky. And as she put out the bed-side lamp, a tender smile crossed her face at Lazar's thoughtfulness in switching it on. It was as though he knew she hadn't wanted to be left in the dark after that awful nightmare.

For another half an hour she lay there, sleep no-where near. A restless feeling possessing her made it impossible to settle to sleep. She lay for some more minutes, then acted on the impulse that came to go to the *salóni* where she could watch the sun come up in all its glory.

Silently, knowing she had already disturbed Lazar's rest too much for one night, she tiptoed out of bed, found her lightweight cotton robe and shrugged into it. Her door made a slight click as she opened it. She held her breath, but heard no other sound.

Her slippered feet whispered along the hall, where daylight filtered in from the wide expanse of glass. Quietly she turned the handle of the door to the *salóni*, and then, 'Oh!' she exclaimed, for the *salóni* was, not as deserted as she fully expected.

Lazar sat there still in his robe as though he had never taken it off after leaving her. A telephone had been plugged in, the base standing on the table she had last seen holding their two empty drinking glasses, the receiving end of the instrument in Lazar's hand.

'I'm sorry,' she said, apologising for interrupting

him, seeing he must be half way through a call. She made to leave, but before she could do so, Lazar had held out an arm inviting her to join him. Hesitating, she watched a warm smile break from him for her, and her feet were taking her to sit beside him on the couch whether he meant she was to sit precisely there or not.

'They are taking their time in answering,' he remarked, his arm stretched along the couch behind her.

'It is a little early,' Clare opined, giving him a smile.

Quite naturally it seemed to her, his arm left the back of the couch and draped over her shoulders. She didn't flinch. She wanted his arm there.

Loosely he held her against him, near to his heart. Then the phone must have been answered, for he was speaking rapidly in Greek, pausing every so often to listen to what was being said at the other end, inserting something of his own. When he replaced the receiver, his call finished, Clare thought for one disappointing moment he was going to take his arm away, but he didn't.

'Can't you sleep either?' he asked softly.

About to tell him she had come to watch the sun come up, she answered only a straightforward, 'No.'

She felt his arm squeeze her shoulders, then he had removed it. 'How about us raiding Phoebe's kitchen? I could do with a drink of something and I'm sure you could.'

Happily Clare went with him, and thought he was the most considerate man she had ever met when instead of making the coffee she was sure he would have preferred, perhaps because he knew of the English and their penchant for tea, it was a cup of tea he placed before her as they sat across from each other at the kitchen table.

She couldn't keep her eyes from straying to the gaping front of his robe, his movements pulling it apart, showing that line of hair which she knew reached down to his navel. Lazar must have followed her look and after that she made sure she looked anywhere but at his chest when quietly he said:

'It disturbs you, Clare, seeing me dressed like this?' She coloured, and couldn't answer, embarrassed to be caught looking at his manly chest. 'I will go and dress,' he said, rising. But Clare had found her voice.

'Oh no, don't,' she said quickly, not wanting anything to break the pleasantness of this impromptu occasion. And when he looked questioningly, 'It's—it's nice sitting here like this.'

'It is, isn't it?' he agreed after a long moment of looking at her, and smiled then as if what she had said pleased him, and sat down again.

Clare had nearly finished her tea, was wondering if she could prolong this lovely interlude by asking for another cup, when he remarked:

'You show no curiosity about whom I was telephoning.'

'I thought it must be business,' she replied, having not thought about his call very much at all, though common sense should have told her he wouldn't be making a business call at that hour—though he could have been contacting someone abroad.

'I telephoned Aeneas,' Lazar told her quietly.

'Aeneas?' she repeated. 'Your brother?' And all at once she was flooded with remorse that in the ten minutes or so they had just spent in easy conversation, not once had she brought up the subject of *her* brother. 'Kit ...' she began, hastily now.

'Aeneas will take your brother to Athens this morning.'

Alarm, fears for Kit had her stopping him from adding anything else. 'You won't—he won't—the punishment you ...' She couldn't bring it out.

'I cannot punish you, Clare.' His face was no longer smiling, 'You, I think, know that. I realise now that I know what I do about you that I have already made you suffer more than I can bear to think about.'

'No, Lazar,' she denied, doubly aware now of his sensitivity.

He ignored her denial and would have spoken again, but it was coming through to her that if he couldn't punish her, then it must mean that Kit still had to be punished—and Lazar had stated at one time that he intended to do that personally.

'You are going to Athens too, aren't you?' she said woodenly.

He nodded, his expression changing. 'I shall meet Aeneas and your brother at my parents' home.'

Suddenly her voice was choked with fear. 'Lazar,' she begged urgently, her voice husky, 'don't—don't hurt Kit. Please say you won't harm him!'

She had hoped never to see that hard cold look on him again, for he had been so kind to her that her imagination had had her believing they had gone past such things. But the coldness in him, the hardness in him, was there in his expression, and he was all proud Greek as he replied:

'I will deal fairly with him.'

With that she had to be satisfied. His look told her she could plead from now until forever, but that her brother would receive exactly what was due. She felt sick at heart. All her enjoyment of spending this time with Lazar had gone. He refused to believe his sister would tell a lie to her parents, so that could only mean that whatever Kit said would be regarded as untrue. Where was the fairness in that?

'Lazar,' a request sprang from her, 'let me come too.' Perhaps she would be allowed to put in a word on Kit's behalf—it wouldn't be for the want of trying if she couldn't. But she discovered Lazar had no intention of taking her to Athens with him.

'No, Clare,' he said stiffly, 'I think not.'

'But why? I . . .'

'It will be too—unpleasant for you.'

Unpleasant? Oh God, poor Kit! Clare went right off the idea of having a second cup of tea. She stood up, not at all surprised that Lazar didn't look regretful at her move. He still had that proud Greek look about him.

'I think I'll go back to my room,' she said coolly, finding she had a pride of her own.

'I have said I will treat your brother fairly, Clare,' he said, his attitude unbending, so that she found no comfort in his words if that was his intention. 'Try to get some sleep.'

Without speaking again, Clare left him, her thoughts with Kit and what was going to happen to him. Lazar had repeated that he would treat him fairly, but what was fair? She didn't for a moment think he would hear what Kit had to say and then tell him in that courteous way he had with him sometimes that everything was all right and that they could both go home. *Go home!*

Those two words had the power to take all other thoughts from her mind. Go home! The words shattered her. She *didn't* want to go home! But she must.

She must want to go home, she thought, trying to ignore what was in her heart.

Stunned, the truth spinning round in her head, she flopped to sit on her bed. No amount of telling herself she *must* want to return to England worked. The truth was still there. This part of Greece had stolen a small part of her heart, the rest had all been stolen by—Lazar! She didn't want to leave. She wanted to stay—with him.

Vacantly her eyes stared into space. What a blind fool she had been! Her love for Lazar had been there for days now, how could she have missed seeing it? How could she stop it? She couldn't, she realised. She was so deeply in love with Lazar Vardakas that she wanted never to leave him.

Absolutely wretched, she was forced to face the fact that she was in love with a man who with his strict code of honour was ready to use physical violence on her brother, maim him for life most likely. Oh, how could she love such a man?

Despair had her throwing herself face down on her bed, her pain too searing for tears. Even if at the very best they were lucky and Kit came out of this without a bruise, she knew complete and utter hopelessness in the knowledge that Lazar would never come to care for her.

Feeling flattened by her frayed emotions, Clare eventually left her bed, the idea with her to have a quick shower, dress and once more ask Lazar to take her with him. Though as she stood under the shower she admitted that her need for him to take her with him was tinged with wanting to spend as much time as she could in his company, suspecting that whichever way the confrontation with Kit went, very soon she would be saying goodbye to Lazar for ever.

Shock and disappointment hit her, however, when she went to look for Lazar. For she found only Phoebe, who to her dismay signed to her that he had already left.

That Saturday was the longest Saturday in Clare's life. Food was out of the question; to eat when heaven knew what was happening in Athens made her stomach rise up just to think of eating.

She did not move from the villa, pinning her hopes on the thought that surely, knowing how worried she must be, that courtesy of Lazar's would have him picking up the phone to tell her what had happened.

Throughout those long waiting hours, just as if she knew what she was going through, Phoebe served her tea and coffee at regular intervals. But at half past four Clare could stand to be indoors no longer. She was convinced as she made her way down to the beach that he would not be phoning now. Her thoughts were not happy as she wandered away from the villa, scenery she had found so breathtaking ignored.

She was still on the beach half an hour later when she came out of her reverie of misery, and the sound of a car coming down the drive penetrated. Then she was racing across the sand without giving thought to the fact that it could well be someone other than Lazar.

Tearing round the side of the villa, she stopped dead. There were two men walking from the car towards the terrace, neither of whom was Lazar. Fleetingly her mind picked up that one of the men, not so tall and thicker set than Lazar, bore some resemblance to the man she loved. But that was all that had time to register. For the other man, lanky with a thatch of blond hair and appearing to be all in one piece with not a mark on him, had a dam bursting inside her and she was running to fling herself at him.

'Kit, oh, Kit!' she cried, her relief too great to be borne.

Kit hugged her to him, but only briefly before pushing her away as if needing to see for himself how she had fared.

'He said you were all right,' he said quickly. 'Are you, Clare? Did he ...'

'I'm fine, fine,' she hastened to assure him. 'Lazar,' she added, knowing it was Lazar Kit must be speaking of, 'Lazar behaved perfectly.' She wiped her eyes, and gave him a happy smile to add weight to her assurances. 'But how about you? Are you ...'

'Physically not a scratch,' Kit shrugged. 'But this whole thing has been a nightmare. There was no way I could get off that damned island even if I had any idea where to find you. I've been ... Well, it doesn't matter about me. Are you sure you're all right?'

Again Clare was at pains to assure him that no harm had befallen her—her aching heart was her secret. And then she became aware how rude she must appear to the man standing beside Kit waiting politely for brother and sister to get their greetings over.

Kit followed the direction of her eyes, then as though he was not certain she would care to be introduced to another Greek as long as she lived, the good manners of his own upbringing had him introducing Lazar's brother, Aeneas Vardakas.

Without hesitation, though her manner was shy as it always was with strangers, Clare extended her hand. Aeneas, a smiling man, took it and shook it warmly.

'Er—Lazar didn't come back with you?' she asked,

trying not to let either man see how important the answer was to her.

'We flew to Thessaloniki together,' Aeneas told her, 'but Lazar went from the airport to visit our uncle. He is in hospital,' he thought to add.

'Oh yes,' said Clare, and then Kit, to her dismay, was telling her:

'A flight has been arranged for us for later this evening.'

'Tonight?' she exclaimed, her heart somewhere down in her boots, though not knowing what else she had expected.

'No point in hanging around,' Kit gave his opinion.

'Of course not,' she replied, and needing to be alone, suspecting there were more tears to come, 'I'll—er—go and pack.'

The three of them walked on to the terrace, Aeneas saying he would go and see about some refreshments.

'Not for me,' Kit stopped him. 'I'll go and talk to Clare while she's packing.'

Clare led the way to her room, fighting against her inner feelings. But she was just not up to answering any of the questions Kit was ready to put to her as she got out her suitcase and began to fill it.

'Won't you tell me what happened in Athens today, Kit?' she forestalled his first question of what on earth was Bruce thinking of letting her come away with a stranger. 'It's been a terrible day for me, waiting, not knowing if you were ...'

'All right, love.' Kit shelved his own enquiries, Clare's peace of mind as always being his first thought. 'Though where to begin ...' He thought for a second or two, then said, 'Well, you know I'd been accused of

getting Sophronia drunk and then—er—seducing her?'
He looked quickly at her to see how she was taking
such talk, prepared to clam up if she looked in any
way upset.

'Yes, Lazar told me. But I told him you wouldn't have
done that unless she was willing.'

Kit looked his thanks. 'Right. Well, I'll scrub round
the fact that I nearly went bonkers with worrying about
you, and get round to this morning when Aeneas had
mobilised the boat and said we were going to Athens.
We went to this architect's dream of a place where his
parents live—the parents kept out of sight, by the way.
But that lying madam Sophronia was there.'

'Sophronia!' Clare exclaimed, having given some
thought to the girl during the day, but never having
thought for a second that Lazar would put her anywhere near Kit again.

'Mm,' Kit confirmed. 'As soon as I saw her I began to
feel easier, though I still didn't know that they weren't
going to give me a going over. But when I saw her I
realised Lazar Vardakas was determined to get to the
truth.'

'But—but he was so certain she hadn't lied,' Clare
put in, remembering he had not even deigned to con-
sider the possibility before.

'I thought it looked that way too to begin with,' Kit
mused. 'I certainly came in for the cold haughty treatment as he looked down his nose and insisted I re-
peat to him what I'd already told Aeneas a hundred
times.'

'About the way you took Sophronia back to that
flat?'

'It doesn't sound too good, does it? I admitted that
myself. But as they say, circumstances alter cases.'

'What were the circumstances, Kit?'

He gave her a friendly grin. 'Here goes, for the hundred and second time,' he said, then after a pause, 'I was minding my own business walking by some derelict buildings when I heard someone crying. By the time I traced the sound the crying was louder and there was this girl sitting breaking her heart on some crumbly old steps. Well, I just couldn't walk away, could I? I mean, anything could have happened to her—er—if you follow me.'

Clare didn't have to follow him, she was right there beside him. Since he had for years now sheltered and protected her, it came as second nature to him, and with her not being there his kindness had extended to cover Sophronia.

'She was sitting in the pitch dark and would say very little, though it was a relief to discover she could speak English. I asked her if I could escort her home, but she then became semi-hysterical, so knowing how the Greeks think of their women's virtue—Pete Nolan warned me to be careful before I came away—God, how I wish I'd taken his advice!—anyway, with her getting hysterical at the thought of going home, I thought the worst had happened to her.'

'That she'd been attacked,' Clare said quietly.

Kit nodded, then hurriedly skated over that to continue, 'I wasn't sure what to do for the best then, but decided her family probably wouldn't want the police involved, so I just sat talking to her, trying to calm her down. I told her anything that came into my head —that I was on holiday, about Mum and Dad, my home in England, Bruce, my job, and about you. Oh, how I wish I'd kept silent about you!' he broke off to say with feeling. 'Anyway, she seemed to grow less hysterical when I told her about my sister, so I talked on and on about you, thinking it would give her confidence in me to know how much we cherish you. I sought to give her the idea that if we cared so much for our Clare it was highly unlikely I would harm any girl in any way.'

Clare felt tears prick her eyes. 'So you eventually gained her confidence?'

'Yes, after what seemed hours. Anyway, I tentatively suggested again that she go home. But that seemed to undo all the good work I'd done. Well, we couldn't sit out there all night if what I thought had happened to her proved the case, so I thought I'd better do something about getting her medical attention. There was a phone in the flat, plus a bottle of brandy I'd bought that morning to take home to Dad. She seemed to like the idea of going back to the flat better than going home anyway. And once there I could see she hadn't been beaten up the way you had been and I was relieved about that, revising my opinion that somebody had set about her. But she was still in a state, so after asking her age and being told she was eighteen, I cracked the brandy open, then chatted to her some more, and eventually she grew calm enough for me to again suggest she go home. She wouldn't let me go with her, but used the phone to ring for a taxi.'

'And that was the end of it as far as you thought.'

'Right. I went back to the flat after seeing her into the taxi, took another swig of brandy, telling myself I'd get Dad another bottle, and went to bed. Then the next thing I know it's three o'clock in the morning and two heavies are tipping me out of bed, packing my gear and dumping me on a boat.'

'You told Lazar all this?' asked Clare.

'In between his interruptions—yes. I soft-pedalled on the bits about you. But I got the shock of my life when he laid into Sophronia—strewth, what a temper he's got!—and he let out that he knew all about you. I couldn't believe you'd told him, we'd never been able to get you to say anything to us about that night.'

There was a question in Kit's voice. Clearly he wanted to know how a stranger to the family had got her to unlock that dark door. But Clare was much more interested to know how it had come about that Lazar had lost his temper with Sophronia to answer that unvoiced question.

'You say Lazar laid into Sophronia?'

'And how!' Kit replied. 'That was the first indication I had that I wasn't going to end up looking like a road traffic accident. She never said a word all the time I'd been telling my side of it, just sat there with a sulky expression on her face. Aeneas was in the room too, but he'd kept quiet and left all the talking to his elder brother. Then when I'd finished speaking, Lazar asked me if I would swear all I had said was true, and I said, "On Clare's life if need be", then without a word he turned to Sophronia and asked what she had to say.'

'And,' Clare prompted, wanting to know how it had all been resolved, 'What did Sophronia say?'

'At first, nothing. Her sulky expression had by this time changed to one of mulishness and I thought then she looked so stubborn he would never get her to change her story. But, quietly to start with, he asked her if she still maintained it had all happened as she had told her father. She didn't speak then, but just nodded her head. Then quietly again he asked her if she didn't think in that case that I should be punished. I don't mind telling you, Clare, I had visions of being set upon and swallowed hard a couple of times before she raised her head and looked about to protest. But nothing came of it and she kept dumb.'

'Didn't she . . .' Clare began.

'Not a word did she say,' Kit told her. 'I protested none too quietly that she was a liar and was told in no uncertain terms to be quiet. And then to my amazement he was telling her he didn't believe a word of what she had told her parents, going to stand over her and telling her that as soon as he'd word from Aeneas of what had happened he'd gone to collect her seducer's sister. "I took her to my villa with the sole intention of doing to her what had been done to you," he said. Then all hell broke loose, Clare. I jumped out of my chair, ready to hit him for what he'd been going to do to you, Aeneas was on his feet pushing me back into my seat before I could land a blow, Sophronia had started to cry and Lazar lost his temper. I heard him putting the boot in by asking how she would feel to have it on her conscience as he would have done for the rest of his life had he carried out his intent and damaged a girl who had once in her life already learned that men could be beasts. I was so shaken to hear that you must have told him what happened to you when you were fourteen that I just sat there stunned. Then as though it was too much for him to remember to speak in English with his temper shot, he launched into a tirade of Greek that had Sophronia spilling everything out in the same language.'

'So you don't know what her side of the story was,' Clare gasped, her packing, almost completed, having been forgotten about for some time.

'Oh yes. He waited until she'd come to a sobbing finish, then with his voice like ice, he said, "In English now, please. That is the least you owe Mr Harper." '

'He made her tell it again?'

'Every word. Though by the time she'd finished, I was feeling more sorry for her than anything else.'

Clare smiled softly. Kit's heart was like butter. Despite all that had happened, he could still find it in his heart to be sorry for the weeping girl. Though she found it in her own heart to feel sorry for her when Kit went on to say:

'Apparently her father had made several attempts to get her married—it's the custom in Greece for the families to do the arranging. But Sophronia wasn't buying it. Aeneas told me on the way here that she's mixed up with a growing movement of feminists in Greece. Anyway, young Sophronia had decided she wanted a career first, and only when *she* was ready a husband, one of her *own* choosing.'

'Oh dear,' said Clare, able to imagine the conflict that must have warred inside the Greek girl, conflict that must have been pretty strong for her to want to flout her country's traditions.

'Oh dear is right,' Kit grimaced. 'It all came to a head that night I came across her. Vardakas senior had taken her to task, telling her she had to conform and that the following evening the man who was to be her future husband was coming with his parents to dine.'

'Sophronia was upset about that,' Clare guessed.

'And then some! Her father had put his foot down pretty firmly, from what I can gather—Aeneas told me too that because she was such a late arrival—he was sixteen when she was born, Lazar eighteen—they'd all spoilt her to death. But this time no one seemed likely to let her wind them round her little finger. There must have been one hell of a row which ended with Mr Vardakas refusing to budge and Sophronia dashing out of the house almost beside herself with the frustration of it all.'

'And that was when you met her?'

'I wish I never had,' said Kit, his face grim for a moment. 'Anyway, by the time she arrived back home, her parents were nearly hairless with the worry of wondering where she'd got to. They then proceeded to put her through the third degree, ranting at her to tell them where she'd been. She's a stubborn cuss, as I saw for myself before Lazar got to work on her, and refused to tell them anything. That was until her father dropped out that anything could have happened to her, and then she had the brilliant idea of saying she'd been seduced, knowing that no man of good family would want to marry her after that.'

'And so leaving her free to have her own way after all,' Clare inserted, having followed everything Kit was telling her very closely.

'Exactly. To her credit she had no intention of telling them where to find me, though for authenticity she'd dropped out my name. What she'd reckoned without, though, was that her father would trace the taxi firm and through them—me.' Kit paused reminiscently. 'She was crying buckets by the time she'd finished repeating all this, but her two brothers were immune to her tears.'

Clare could just imagine the scene, could imagine the proud look Lazar would wear, his face cold at the shame Sophronia had brought to them all by her lies.

'What happened then?' she asked.

'Lazar made her apologise, and then,' Kit paused a moment before going on, 'and then he asked to see me privately.'

Poor Lazar, Clare couldn't help thinking. His pride must have suffered a severe blow. He would want to see Kit privately to give him his own full apology, and maybe assure him that he had not carried out his threat to seduce her.

'Come on, Clare, let's get out of here,' said Kit, seeing from her solemn face that she looked near to tears herself, but with no idea that her heart was bleeding for the way Lazar must have felt.

'Nearly ready,' she said, forcing a bright note.

Kit strolled out with her case as Clare took one last look round the room, her eyes coming to rest on the communicating door. She had a real battle against tears then. Oh, if only she'd had the nerve to go through that door! She would at least have that to remember. Instinct told her Lazar would have been patient with her, and she remembered her feelings when his hand had touched her naked breast, and she—she would have given him her all. Too late now. Too late ...

CHAPTER EIGHT

BECAUSE Aeneas was there, Kit did not have an opportunity to put any questions to Clare. And as she sat with her brother in the rear seat of the car as Aeneas drove them to the airport, Clare was too upset by the thought that she had already said goodbye to Lazar, that she had no information she wanted to volunteer.

It seemed impossible that she would never see Lazar again. Her broken heart cried out for just one more chance to see him—just once more, that was all she asked. Yet she knew he wouldn't be there at the airport to see them off. Even if his pride had not taken that bitter blow of knowing his sister had lied, she couldn't think he would come away from the hospital after seeing his uncle just for the purpose of seeing her off.

Her mind went back to how friendly he had been with her that morning, the way he had sat on the couch with his arm around her, the way he had made her a cup of tea. Dear heaven, they had been friends then, she knew it. Oh, if only she had known then that it was the last time she was to see him, she wouldn't have stalked off with her cool pride.

She came out of the sadness of her thoughts to find Aeneas had turned the car into the approach road of the airport. It was foolish of her to scan her eyes looking for the Mercedes convertible, for it wasn't there, but she freely admitted that love had made a nonsense of logic.

'If you will come this way, Clare.' Aeneas spoke gently at her side, and because he was the brother of Lazar, she smiled at him.

Between them Kit and Aeneas carried the luggage and she was left with Kit while Aeneas went to check on the arrangements.

'You look a bit peaky, Clare,' Kit observed. 'Are you sure you're feeling all right?'

She would have to make an effort to cheer up, she saw, her mind having been far away wondering if she could ask Aeneas to say goodbye to Lazar for her. 'I'm fine, Kit,' she said, and lied, 'Looking forward to getting home.'

'And so say all of us!' was Kit's heartfelt reply.

Aeneas returned, a pile of magazines beneath his arm which he gave to Clare with the comment, 'Perhaps these will save the journey from being too tedious for you, Clare.'

Thanking him for his kindness, she took the magazines from him, thinking that Aeneas too had a share of the same charm she had seen in Lazar from time to time. It was on the tip of her tongue to try and form some message for him to give to his brother, but shyness held her quiet for a moment too long, and by that time Aeneas had turned to Kit and was telling him that if they went through to the departure lounge their plane would be ready to take off.

He shook hands with Clare first, wishing her a pleasant flight, then turned to shake hands with Kit. A sudden jostle of people next to Clare had her separated from her brother. She knew he must have thought she had already gone through as she saw him disappear. Aeneas must have thought so too, for looking to give him a last smile she saw him going in the opposite direction.

As she was about to turn to go through to the departure lounge, her eyes widened and she stood rooted. For there, having spotted her snowy head straight away and coming towards her, was Lazar.

She knew her colour was high, but try as she might nothing would get the smile she wanted to come. Lazar too, she saw when he reached her, was unsmiling. He stood looking down at her and the thought winged to her mind that years seemed to have been added to him since she had seen him last early that morning.

'Lazar, I . . .' she began, wanting to tell him not to be upset because of what Sophronia had done. But the words stuck, and it came to her that his pride would prefer she didn't mention it. 'I'm—I'm glad you came,' she said instead. And when he just continued to look at her as though wanting to photograph her image, which just showed how badly he affected her, she thought, blaming love for the idiot she had become, she added, 'I wouldn't have wanted to go without saying goodbye to you.'

'You forgive me, then, Clare?' he asked, his voice sounding tightly in check.

'Forgive you!'

'Kit has told you Sophronia lied.'

Her smile broke. 'Oh, Lazar, of course I forgive you,' she exclaimed, feeling there would be nothing to forgive if only he would smile in return.

'Your heart is much too tender,' he said, his voice softening, but with no smile for her. 'You are about to take off.'

It was a statement, no answer needed, but she replied, 'Yes.' She knew she had to turn and leave him, but she felt too choked to utter another word, afraid she might shake him rigid by begging him to let her stay.

Some part of her had her holding out her hand to him in a movement to shake hands, but it seemed to her she had no part in the formal gesture. Afraid that any minute now her face would crumple, she looked at his hands down by his sides, for he had made no move to take her hand in his. Shaken, she saw his fists were clenched and knew that it had taken a lot for him to hang on to his pride and come to say goodbye to her.

She was no longer smiling when her eyes met his. She let her hand fall. 'Goodbye, Lazar,' she said quietly, and went to turn away.

And then, to her utter amazement—and joy—Lazar's

two hands came up to stay her as he took her by the shoulders, and the next moment she was in his arms.

'*Hérete, karthia mou,*' he said thickly, his voice sounding so agonised, so disturbed, that involuntarily she was jerking backwards out of his arms and standing white-faced to stare at him. She had no idea what he had said, but there was so much emotion in his voice she just had to look at him to see if her ears had played her false.

They had. Imagination, damned imagination again, she thought as she stood speechlessly looking at him. For there was no emotion to be seen, agonised, disturbed or otherwise, as taut-cheeked he looked into her shocked eyes. And then he took a step back and without waiting another second, without so much as another glance at her, he turned swiftly about and strode determinedly away.

They had been in the air some ten minutes before Clare was able to put any reason into her imaginings of her parting from Lazar. Oh God, she groaned, what an idiot she was! Why couldn't she just have accepted his embrace of parting as that given only from a man who had seen her through a few emotional crises?—her first kiss, her nightmare, to name but two. He had intended, she saw now, that they should part as friends. And what had she done but jumped back out of his arms as though she was still afraid of men, still afraid of him.

Kit asking her how in the world she had managed to trick Bruce into leaving, and why had she done so, had her setting her mind to work in other directions to tell him how it had come about.

She was glad to have Kit with her on that flight, glad that he found so many questions to ask, all of which needed an answer, for at least it kept her from thinking solely of the growing miles separating her from Lazar.

It was she who suggested they shouldn't tell their parents anything of what had happened, and when Kit looked doubtful, following up what she had told him of her feeling guilty that the whole family considered her before they considered themselves, hence her lying to him so he like Bruce should have a holiday on his own, she added:

'It will only worry them, make them wonder if it's sent me more into myself, and it hasn't, Kit, honestly it hasn't. Couldn't we just tell them that both you and I went to the flat Peter Nolan booked in Athens?'

Kit thought about it for some minutes, then, 'Perhaps you're right. It would worry them to know what's happened—it wouldn't be a very nice homecoming, would it?'

August gave way to September, September to October, and not a day passed when Clare did not think of Lazar. She had heard nothing of him—not that she expected to, but that didn't make it any easier to bear.

The family were all together again, their holidays mostly forgotten. Bruce had returned after thoroughly enjoying his time spent potholing, and her parents had returned looking much more relaxed for their break.

Over the next few months after their return, they all began to notice small changes in Clare, each change noted with small apprehension and a great deal of pleasure. For all there were times when she sat quietly, a faraway look in her eyes, there were red letter days like the day she took the Mini into town and came home with a whole range of cosmetics she thought she would like to try, the day she tried out a different hair-style before deciding she liked her old style best. Small things, admittedly, but to her family who had seen her through the days when she had been afraid of her own shadow, they were things that gave them all a lift. The night Clare went to bed and for the first time closed her bedroom door behind her had them anxiously looking at each other. But when the next night and the night after that the same thing happened, they began silently to rejoice. Was she losing her fear of the dark?

Apprehension and pleasure were about of equal mix the day she told them she had accepted an invitation to go to the cinema with Bruce's friend Rob Edmonds.

Clare silently admitted she was a little apprehensive about her date herself. She had no special feelings for Rob, Lazar held all of those, but in bringing her to life Lazar had awakened in her a curiosity to learn more of the everyday things that went on in the world.

The night Rob called for her, Bruce, seemingly casual, went to let his friend in, but it was some minutes before they both came into the sitting room. The protection her family had practised was still there, then? Clare had no doubts that Bruce had been telling Rob not to try anything with her, probably threatening what he would personally do to him if he did.

Shyly—perhaps she would always be shy; she didn't know—she sat beside Rob in his car; shyly she had sat beside him in the cinema. He behaved perfectly and after the film brought her straight back home, not attempting to stop on the way or try to kiss her at her door. She hadn't wanted him to, and as her confidence grew she agreed to go out with him another couple of times. On the last of these outings he had attempted to kiss her, but her sharply called out 'Don't!' as she struggled out of arms that didn't fit stopped him, brought forth an apology plus the revelation that Bruce had told him of her deep-rooted shyness, but that she was so sweet he had forgotten himself.

Clare had gone into the house knowing she had not been afraid when Rob's arms had come round her. She wasn't afraid of being kissed by him either. It was just that loving Lazar so much she had felt compelled to call out 'Don't!' wanting no one's mouth on hers but his.

October gave way to November, and still there was no let-up in her heartache. Conversation began to be of Christmas, preparations to be made, shopping to be done. And it was on the last Saturday in November when Clare had gone with Kit to select something suitable for a child to give for the raffle at the village Christmas Fayre, that as Kit went to pay for the construction set which he said would be suitable for a boy or girl since girls were into such things now, Clare stood near a display of dolls in the toy department while waiting for him to be served.

She was glancing idly along the display when suddenly one doll stood out from all the rest. A small 'Oh!' left her involuntarily as she gazed at the doll beautifully arrayed in Greek national costume, oblivious to the fact that Kit had come to join her, the memories seeing the doll evoked taking her to that far-off land.

'Hmmp.' Kit's grunt had her coming out of her trance. 'Greeks!' he muttered disparagingly, and piloted her out of the store.

They were back in the car before another word was

said, but she had been thinking as they walked along. The disparaging way Kit had said 'Greeks' was painful to her. She didn't want him to feel that way.

'Kit,' she said quickly before he could start the engine, 'was it so very bad for you on Niakos? I mean ...' Her voice faded as he turned to look at her. Poor Kit, he'd had a tough time, how could she expect him to have fond memories of the place of his incarceration?

'Well,' he said thoughtfully, covering his surprise that she had brought the subject up, 'in all honesty, it was a beautiful place. But I was going off my head with worrying about you too much to enjoy it. Though in all fairness, once they'd dumped me on the boat I was treated with courtesy, cold though it was.'

He leaned forward to switch on the ignition, ready to leave the conversation there. But Clare didn't want to leave it there. She suspected he was nursing a grievance against Lazar and wanted him to see something of the quality of the man that she herself had seen.

'Don't start the car yet, Kit,' she stopped him, and stumbled on when she saw she had his attention. 'L-Lazar was very kind to me,' she told him, bringing Lazar's name out with difficulty, for all she had no such trouble the times she had spoken his name out loud in the privacy of her room.

'Kind?'

'Yes,' Clare said quickly, eager to disabuse Kit's mind that the man she loved was any sort of a villain. 'I had a nightmare one night—Lazar was marvellous to me.' She heard an exclamation break from Kit that she had suffered one of her nightmares without anyone of the family there to help her afterwards, but an exclamation broke from her own lips as a sudden realisation hit her. 'Hey!' she said, 'I haven't had that nightmare since I came home.'

'Neither you have,' said Kit with equal surprise. 'Three months, Clare—that must be a record!'

They were each silent for a moment or two, Clare reflecting how much she had to be grateful to Lazar for. She had changed mightily, all for the better, since her return from his country.

Kit too must have been having similar thoughts, for he said, 'It would appear he's been able to do something for you none of your family have been able to achieve.'

'You've all been wonderful to me,' she said gently. 'I shall never be able to thank you, Bruce, Mum and Dad for the way you've sheltered me all these years.'

It was a sensitive moment, and her love for her family welled up within her.

'Not everyone has such a lovely sister,' Kit said gruffly, then went on, 'Perhaps that Lazar Vardakas chap wasn't such a bad bloke after all. He certainly got that lying Sophronia singing like a canary!'

Clare grinned at Kit's expression for Sophronia, revealing all there was to know. But her grin disappeared when Kit went on absently, almost as if he had forgotten she was sitting beside him!

'He needn't have offered to marry you either, but he did.'

'*Marry me!*' The exclamation shot from her. 'You mean . . .' her voice started to peter out as incredulity took it. 'You mean Lazar said he would marry me?'

Kit mistook the hoarseness in her voice for another reason. 'Now don't get in a stew! I told him "No, thank you" on your behalf. I didn't mean to let anything slip, but you've been so different recently from the way you were I've rather got out of the habit of watching that I don't say anything that might upset you.'

Kit was underlining again what she already knew, the extent of her family's caring for her. But just at that moment the conversation Lazar must have had with him in Athens when he had asked Kit to see him privately was overcoming her undying gratitude to her family.

'I thought he wanted to see you privately to apologise formally,' she said, a riot going on inside her. 'But ...'

'Oh, he apologised too, without reservation. But when he began asking when would our parents be home so he could come and speak to my father about you, I told him I was acting on my father's behalf and anything he wanted to say to Dad could be said to me —so he brought up this marriage thing. But there's no need for you to worry, love. He goes a bundle on this honour business, so I expect he thought it the only decent thing he could do since according to his way of thinking he'd compromised you.'

Kit was probably right, Clare thought, yet she couldn't leave it there. They had been back three months now and this was the first time they had discussed what had happened. She couldn't wait that long again to find out more.

'Er—what did Lazar say, when you said "No, thank you"?' She chewed at her bottom lip. 'I mean, did he just accept it with a sigh of relief?'

'Look, Clare, do you want to discuss it?' Kit replied, looking disturbed at having said too much already.

'Yes, I want to discuss it,' she said firmly. 'I'm no longer the terrified mouse I used to be, Kit.'

Kit was silent for a while as he considered her answer.

'All right then,' he said at last. 'I expected him to accept my refusal on your behalf, I must admit. As I saw it he could well think his honour satisfied by having made the offer.' He looked at her briefly as though to gauge if she was up to hearing the rest, then saw a determination on her face with no sign of panic. 'But he didn't. He then challenged me to give him a reason for my refusal.'

'Oh,' said Clare, careful not to let Kit see the agitation that was going on in her insides. A glimpse of that would have him clamming up straight away. 'So,' oh, she could sound casual, though how she could when this was so tremendously important defied belief, 'so what reason did you give him?'

'Well ...' Kit hesitated. 'Well, he must have seen how shy you were, for one thing. And you've said yourself how he looked after you when you had a nightmare —God, I'll bet your screams frightened the life out of him! They used to me. Was that when you told him the cause of your nightmares?'

Kit had to accept that it was without her answering; Clare was more anxious for him to get to the nub of the matter than to want to introduce a side issue conversation.

'Go on, Kit, do,' she begged, trying to hide her impatience.

'Well, knowing all that, it couldn't have come as any great surprise when I told him how ill you'd been and that our aunt, your doctor, had said that ...' Again he hesitated.

'Kit, if you don't hurry up and tell me I shall go and ask Aunt Katy myself to tell me whatever it is you're struggling with!' Clare burst out, her impatience getting the better of her.

'I'm not supposed to tell you,' Kit defended, then added, 'but since you're miles better than you were—here goes. Aunt Katy told us that there was little possibility that you would ever marry, that she doubted you would ever be a wife in the full sense of the word to any man.' Clare blanched at that, before realising that until three months ago she would have gone along with that prognosis.

'Carry on,' she said, keeping the shock of what she had just heard from her voice. 'What else did she say?'

'She said that even if you did marry it must only be to a man who would love you so much he would know how to be gentle with you when—well, you know.'

'What else, Kit?' Clare asked again, her voice deliberately even, sensing there was more.

'She said that the man must be right for you, that he must love you so much that he would put you before himself. But more than that, you must love him in the same way too, because—because if you didn't then you could go right back to the way you were—or—worse.'

Kit finished telling her what Aunt Katy had said, an apologetic note in his voice as though he regretted having told her.

'You—you told Lazar all this?' Clare questioned quietly after a moment.

'Yes.'

'And what did he say?'

'Nothing. Not one single solitary word. It was as though what I'd told him finished the conversation about marriage. He went and looked out of the window for about a minute, then when he turned around told me that you and I were welcome to stay at his villa for as long as we liked, that he wouldn't be there, and when I said no, that I wanted to get you home all right away, he then proceeded to make flight arrangements to Salonika and from Salonika home.'

Alone in her room that night, Clare went over everything Kit had revealed to her. Oh, how she wished he had left her to do her own answering to Lazar's proposal! Her answer wouldn't have been 'No, thank you'. She turned away from the fantasy. How could she have said yes? That wouldn't have been fair to Lazar, with his proposal only being made because his proud Greek honour demanded it.

What if his reasons for wanting to marry her weren't motivated solely by honour, though? For a good ten minutes she went into a dream world of his wanting to marry her being because he loved her. That he had accepted Kit's reasons for there being no chance of such a match because he did not know that she loved him, and that he loved her enough to put her before his wish to have her as his wife because he was afraid of what it might do to her.

Clare slept only fitfully that night, though she had no terrifying nightmare to add to her unrest. She rather thought that nightmares were a thing of the past and got up the next morning, her thoughts still with Lazar. During the afternoon, on the pretext of having something she wanted to do in her room, she went upstairs and dissected everything Lazar had ever said to her.

She recalled the time he had made her tell him what had made her so afraid of men. 'It's important to me— to both of us,' he had said. Was it as she had believed, then, because with honour demanding to be satisfied he could not make her be the one to pay if there was some good reason for her fear—or, dared she think it, because he had to know for their future happiness? Could he possibly have meant he had to know why she was afraid so that he could take steps to ensure she was never afraid of him?

Coming to her senses, Clare discounted her thoughts as pure dreams, a product of her lively imagination. And yet, as she lay in bed that night, it came back to her as it had many times since, the way in which they had parted at Micra Airport. '*Hérete, karthia mou,*' he had said, his voice full of emotion. Oh God, why had she backed out of his arms as though his tight hold had frightened her to death?

Her mother was bright and cheerful when Clare went downstairs the next morning. 'Let's forget household chores today,' she told Clare. 'We'll pack these men off to work and spend the morning in Guildford.'

Clare fell in with her mother's plans, and no sooner was the breakfast washing up out of the way than they were in the Mini heading for town, her mother reminding her of the new dress they had discussed as her Christmas present.

'It will be nice for you to have something new to wear on Christmas Day,' Ruth Harper told her daughter as they stood in the cobbled High Street in Guildford wondering which store to go in first. 'Though,' her manner teasing, 'if we do get it today, don't you dare wear it until the twenty-fifth!'

Clare did see the dress she would like, and saw too a pleased smile cross over her mother's features that it was a snugly fitting dress and not at all like the 'bell tents' her wardrobe held.

'Try it on, dear,' she instructed, and when Clare came out of the changing room, 'Oh yes, you must have it!'

It was a dress of fine wool in a deep shade of red, a

colour that complemented her snowy head perfectly. The buttons down to the waist did up to make the bodice fit snugly over her bustline, the below-knee length ending with a flare of tiny pleats that fell from just above her knee.

She looked good in it, Clare had to agree as they left the dress department, her mother firmly taking charge of the carrier bag. She had looked modern, almost sophisticated, she thought, her thoughts taking flight to wish Lazar could see her wearing it—he would just have to change his mind then about her being ashamed of her body. Oh, Lazar . . .

'There's Chloe Rattenbury!' Ruth Harper exclaimed, breaking into Clare's thoughts and taking her with her to meet the other woman half way, Chloe Rattenbury exclaiming:

'Well met! It must be time for elevenses.'

The three of them ambled to the store's lift, the two older women chatting away nineteen to the dozen as though they hadn't seen each other for twelve months and were anxious to catch up on news, for all Clare knew very well her mother had attended Chloe Rattenbury's coffee morning only last week.

It was while they were waiting for the lift to come that the idea Clare had been nursing in her waking hours last night suddenly had to have its way. She knew then she would have no peace from the idea until she knew.

'Mum—Mrs Rattenbury—would you mind very much if I don't join you for coffee? Er—there's something I want to do.'

'Ah,' said Chloe Rattenbury, catching on straight away, or so she thought. 'Come on, Ruth. We'll see you later, Clare.'

'What . . .?' Her mother was obviously bemused.

'It may take me some time,' Clare put in quickly. 'If you're not here I'll go to the car park, I've got my set of keys.'

'But, Clare . . .'

'Come on, Ruth.' Chloe Rattenbury ushered her into the lift, and the lift doors were closing as Clare heard her say, 'Clare obviously wants to get you a surprise Christmas present . . .'

Thinking to get her mother an extra special surprise Christmas present, Clare left the store. Then, her errand urgent now, she almost ran in the direction of the library, taking a short cut down a passage. Somehow or other she just had to find out what those words of Greek were that Lazar had said in parting. She knew she stood to be sorely disappointed, but the way in which he had said them, that ragged emotion in his voice she had put down to her imagination up until a couple of days ago, kept making itself heard over and over again in her head. She just had to know what it was he had said; it seemed vitally important now that she knew he had been prepared to marry her.

Armed with dictionaries and many reference books from the library shelves, Clare sat down to begin her task, discovering very quickly that it was going to be no easy matter. She took many wrong trails in changing a phonetic sound back into the Greek alphabet and then back into English, but she had no intention of giving up until she had the answer she wanted.

How long it took her she had no idea. She had lost all sense of time. But at last she had got it. She had turned '*Hérete, karthia mou*' into English, checked it three times because she just couldn't believe it. And then, when she was absolutely positive she had not made any mistake, she just sat there with a dazed expression on her face, for '*Hérete, karthia mou*', translated, said 'Goodbye, my heart'.

CHAPTER NINE

'GOODBYE, my heart,' came whispering from her, so perhaps it was as well she had the table to herself, though she was oblivious just then to anything save her discovery. What did it mean? Did it mean—her hands began to tremble—did it mean that Lazar's offer to marry her had not been purely because his sense of honour demanded it?

Afraid to think along those lines, too scared at the despairing let-down feeling she would get if she analysed the answer to that and came up with the answer of 'Don't be ridiculous', she reached for the reference books again, her mind struggling to remember the word he had called her when he had cradled her in his arms comforting her after her nightmare. *Agapémene*, that was it! '*Agapémene*. You are safe now.'

More familiar now with the books in front of her, she ploughed through, checking each letter closely, her heart knocking against her ribs when she had the answer. She could take any one of three words from the translation she saw, all of them endearments—beloved, dear, or favourite.

There was no room now to be afraid. She had to think along the lines her mind wanted to go. Could Lazar really want to marry her because—because he loved her? Oh God. She felt faint at the idea, her mind going over again the things he had said, the things he had done. Physically she had thought he desired her, let herself believe it without backing away from the thought as she relived that excitement his touch on her breast had aroused in her that day. She had desired him too.

Yet could he love her? Did he love her? 'Goodbye, my heart,' he had said at the airport. Clare tried to think positive. She hadn't imagined that agony in his voice, she knew she hadn't. But had it been agony that for her sake he had to part from her?

A low groan escaped her at the remembrance of the way she had pulled away from him as though stung when she had heard that thick emotion in his voice. Oh God, she thought, he could have interpreted that as confirming everything Kit had told him as being true. That adult emotion did send her back into herself, that adult emotion did frighten her, that she was too afraid to stay in his arms, was afraid of—him.

She became aware that someone was looking at her peculiarly, wondered if she looked as pale as she felt and awakened to the realisation that her mother would be waiting for her. She returned the books to the shelves and left the library, her feet moving automatically in the direction of where they had left the car, her mind too busy with her thoughts to notice where they were going.

Oh, if only she could let Lazar know that far from making her afraid of him he had started a fire inside her that burned fear to ashes. He had thawed that block of ice that encased her heart, but he would never know it.

It was Monday of the next week, December in its

infancy, that Clare looked at the shadows beneath her
eyes that told their own story of her restless nights and
knew that she would have to do something. She
couldn't go on like this. She was breaking up inside.
Something was goading at her, telling her there was a
chance of happiness for her if only she had the courage to do something about it.

In her room she sat deep in thought for a long time.
She discounted the idea of travelling to Greece to see
Lazar. What could she say when she got there? Always
supposing he was there anyway, travelling as much as
he did he could be anywhere. And anyway, she would
look a fine fool if the whole of it was no more than
a figment of her imagination. It would look well if,
face to face with her, he gave her that cruel look he
had used on her on occasion and scoffed, 'Me in love
with you? May I recommend you to a good psychia-
trist?'

Her thoughts getting on top of her, Clare left her
room. In the hall she put on her coat, then went into
the kitchen in search of her mother.

'Going out, love?' Ruth Harper asked, seeing her
dressed in her outdoor things.

'I'm—er—a Christmas card short. I thought I'd go
to the village—anything I can get you?'

Why she had said that Clare had no idea as, armed
with a small shopping list and a shopping basket, she
walked out of the gate. She had never had to make
excuses to her family before. She saw then that being
in love had made her far more vulnerable than ever
before, made her sensitive to even the smallest enquiry
of 'Going out, love?'

Her face was flushed by the time she reached the
village post office, but it wasn't from the exhilaration

of the half-mile walk. Timid for so long, she knew
the need to be bold had come to her. She had just spent
one year-long week in gathering her courage together.
Now she knew what she was going to do. That lie
about needing a Christmas card had given her the idea.

Inside the post office she purchased a Christmas card,
having had no such intention when she had closed the
garden gate. The card depicted a snow-covered, typic-
ally English scene and she took it with her when she
went to sit on a bench in the bus shelter.

For long moments she stared in front of her, then re-
moving the cellophane wrapping from the card, she
took her pen from her shoulder bag, and using the bag
for something to bear on she leant over and wrote,
'With love, Clare.'

Quickly now in case her courage deserted her, she
wrote Lazar's name and the address of the villa on the
envelope, popped the card inside and sealed it urgently,
hurrying back to the post office with her insides churn-
ing as she waited for the postmistress to tell her how
much the postage was to Greece.

Long, agonising days followed, days when she found
a hundred and one things to cause her anxiety. Would
her card get there? Had she addressed it correctly?
Would Lazar be at the villa to receive it? Perhaps he
only ever went there in the summer? What would he
think if he did get it, did open it? Would he think
her 'With love, Clare' was just the free and easy way
English girls went on? Or, as she was hoping, if he did
love her, would he have learnt enough about her to
know that that was not her way?

She was certain of nothing on those days, apart from
one thing. She had no regrets in having done what she
had. If she never heard from Lazar again, then at least

she had had the courage to do something constructive in finding out one way or another if she meant anything to him.

Clare awoke on Christmas Eve morning, her anticipation in waiting for the postman dimmed. Lazar had had time now to send her a card in return, but nothing had arrived. She was more quiet than usual when she went downstairs to join her mother, the men in the family having gone off early that morning proclaiming that they were busy at the office since they were having an extra day off at the other end of the holiday. Lazar didn't love her, she knew that now. Her pride had been battered into the ground, and she had no idea how she was going to keep her family from knowing she was bleeding inside on this festive occasion.

It was a death knoll blow to all her hopes when the postman, late because of his Christmas deliveries, finally arrived, to hear her mother say, 'Nothing for you, love,' as she inspected the writing on the envelopes in her hand. She had told herself that if there wasn't anything in the post for her this morning, then she could put everything down to her imaginings.

'Coffee, Mum?' she enquired in an attempt to appear as if she hadn't been expecting anything.

'We'll have it in the . . .' Her mother's reply was cut short by the ringing of the telephone. 'I'll get it,' she said, being the nearest to the hall.

Clare put the kettle to boil, having not much interest in who was calling. She wouldn't make the coffee until her mother had finished, though, in case it was Chloe Rattenbury. Her mother could be on the phone for half an hour . . .

'It wasn't Mrs Rattenbury,' she said, attempting to tease when her mother came into the kitchen. Then she noticed she was wearing a slightly puzzled expression. 'What's the matter?'

'The call's for you. He's holding on,' her mother replied.

'He ...' Clare whispered, hope soaring ridiculously.

'I'm not sure,' Ruth Harper said slowly, 'but I think he has just a touch of a foreign accent.'

The cup and saucer Clare was holding crashed unheeded to the floor, tears springing to her eyes. 'Oh, Mum!' she choked, and that was all. Then she was streaking out into the hall.

'Lazar,' she said huskily down the phone; it was unthinkable that it should be anyone else—fate wouldn't be so cruel. No answer came, and she was terrified she had kept him waiting too long and he had hung up. And then his voice came, and tears were streaming down her face and she felt so weak she just had to sit down on the bench adjoining the telephone table.

'I have just arrived at the villa,' he said, his voice stiff, the sound coming through as clear as a bell as she realised he was phoning her from Greece. Then bluntly, getting straight to the point, 'Did you mean what you said on your card?'

A dryness was attacking her throat, making speech difficult. She swallowed painfully. 'Yes,' she said, then, frightened he hadn't heard, for all she was having no trouble hearing him, 'Yes, I did,' she said more loudly.

Her words were answered with an agonising silence. She wished she could see his face. Then he said two short words, as stiff and unbending as when he had first spoken.

'Prove it,' he said.

'Prove it?' How was she to prove it? Didn't he be-

lieve her? And then he was further scattering all her
senses by saying slowly, and deliberately so she
shouldn't misunderstand him at all:

'A car will arrive for you in about an hour from
now. The chauffeur will have instructions to take you
to the airport where a plane will be waiting for you.'

He must have heard her gasp of astonishment, she
thought, for his voice had dipped at the end as though
he was having a hard time controlling it, and while all
she could do was grip tightly on to the phone, shaken
to the very core, his voice came again, fully controlled
as he said slowly:

'Spend your Christmas with me.'

Robbed of speech, her vision blinded, Clare could
only sit there, unable to take it in. Was this happening?
Was this really happening that Lazar was asking her
to ... Apparently he had tired of waiting for her answer,
for as not one word would leave her throat, his voice
came again, roughly this time:

'Will you, Clare?'

And suddenly she was terrified in case he would hang
up if she couldn't find her voice, and mindless of the
family complications, nothing important any more save
giving him his answer, she fought to unlock her paralysed vocal cords.

'Yes, Lazar—I will,' she said, and was left holding the
telephone as he didn't wait to hear any more, but
hung up.

For long seconds she sat stunned, holding the phone
in her hand, going over every word he had spoken.
Then, galvanised into action as she heard him say
again, 'A car will arrive for you in about an hour from
now,' she crashed the receiver back on its rest and went
tearing into the kitchen to find her mother clearing

away broken remains of crockery and had only the vaguest of recollections that she was responsible for the breakage.

'Mum,' she said, tears of happiness rolling down her cheeks. 'Oh, Mum, I'm going to Greece for Christmas!'

'*Greece!*' Ruth Harper was astounded as she promptly put dustpan and brush down, her face showing shock and bewilderment. 'Clare, you ...'

'Please, Mum,' begged Clare, going over to her and pulling at her hands until they were sitting facing each other on kitchen chairs, 'I know this is going to come as a shock to you, but—but please hear what I have to say before you try and stop me.'

Ten minutes later her mother was sitting looking as stunned as Clare had first felt. Considering it would take up too much time to explain how Lazar had collected her from this very house and why, Clare let her mother believe she had met Lazar on her holiday in Greece.

'You've certainly changed since you came back from that holiday,' Mrs Harper said at last. 'We've all noticed it. I was telling your Aunt Katy about you the other day and she said the time had come to let you make your own decisions, but—but Greece!' She broke off to ask, 'Aren't you—afraid of this man?'

'I love him, Mum. With Lazar I'm afraid of nothing.'

Ruth Harper thought about that for a moment, seeing from her daughter's lovely shining eyes the truth of that statement, and yet she couldn't cut out the constant vigil she had kept over her for the last five years just like that.

'You say Kit has met him.'

'Yes.'

'Then let Kit go with you. I can phone him at the ...'

'No, Mum.' Clare smiled gently at her. 'You, Dad and the boys have been wonderful to me, and I'm so grateful. But this is something I have to do on my own. Don't you see that Lazar, knowing all about me, won't truly believe I fear nothing from him unless I go alone?'

'He loves you—this Lazar?'

Clare wished she could say yes. 'I don't know,' she answered, 'But I have to go to him, Mum.'

Seeing her determination, perhaps seeing some of her own determination she had handed down, Ruth Harper got to her feet. 'I suppose if I ring your father to get him to come home to talk to you it wouldn't make any difference to your decision to go, would it?' she asked hopefully.

'No, Mum,' Clare answered quietly.

'In that case we'd better go and get you packed— only promise me one thing, Clare.' Clare was ready to promise anything. 'Promise to ring us as soon as you can.'

Dissatisfied with her wardrobe, Clare had never loved her mother more when as she bent over her suit-case she came into the room carrying the dress that had been kept in her wardrobe until tomorrow.

'I expect you'll want to wear your Christmas present to travel in,' she said.

Sitting, the sole passenger in the executive jet, Clare had to pinch herself to believe it had all happened. Here she was in her lovely red dress, having hugged her mother goodbye and trying not to see the tears in her eyes lest her own tears should start again. She had been chauffeur-driven to the airport and—she checked her watch—in about an hour from now she would be seeing Lazar. Her insides trembled, but try as she might she could think up no words of greeting that wouldn't sound stilted and not at all what she wanted to say.

Disappointment hit her that Lazar was not at the airport in Thessaloniki to meet her, though she over-rode her disappointment and beamed a smile at Rasmus when he, recognising her first, came to relieve her of her case.

In the car she realised she needed the extra time it would take to get to the villa to get herself under con-trol. She was shaking like a leaf, must try and stop won-dering what was going to happen. A terrible thought smote her. What if Lazar thought she had been angling for an invitation to stay at the villa for Christmas when she had sent him that Christmas card? What if he had invited her for no other reason than that he believed he still owed her something? Oh God, what a time to start getting ideas like that, she thought, trying to re-member he had asked her to prove she had meant the 'With love' she had written.

But by the time Rasmus had turned down the drive to the villa, she was so confused she wasn't sure of any-thing any more, save wondering if she was wise to have come at all.

It was on shaky legs that she got out of the car. Rasmus stayed by her side until they were in the hall, and then as though sensing her nervousness since there was still no sign of Lazar—yet he must have heard the car, it was so peaceful and quiet here—he said, '*Tó salóni*,' and she knew then when Rasmus turned and left her, it was in the *salóni* she would find Lazar.

Her hand on the door handle, she had to give a cough to clear her throat, then slowly she turned the handle and pushed the door inwards.

Lazar dominated the room; the room ceased to exist for her as her eyes went straight to him. An overwhelming shyness was constricting her throat as she stood there just inside the door. He was on his feet, a caged look about him as though it was some time since he had sat down. He was dressed all in black but no longer looked like the devil she had once feared. He was as she remembered him—yet not so. Never had he looked so gaunt, so—so as if life had not treated him kindly this past four months.

Her voice frozen, she wanted to rush over to him, to hold him in her arms, to have his arms that did fit, holding her. But the longer she stood there not saying a word, the more taut the expression on his face became, forbidding almost, as in turn those dark eyes searched her face.

In the end it was Lazar who spoke first. 'You came alone?' he enquired stiffly.

'I—Mother wanted Kit to come with me.' She found her voice, hating that it sounded as stiff and as formal as his, and trying her best to find some warmth as she added, 'But—but I wanted to come by myself.'

A look of strain was added to his taut expression. 'I did not think you would come,' he said, his voice no warmer than hers for all her efforts.

'I . . .' Clare stopped.

Oh, this was awful! They were like strangers. Did he feel it too? Worse—did he think of her as a stranger? She chewed at her bottom lip, half way to wishing she had never come. Courage, Clare, she mentally brought herself up short. Have you come all this way just to go crashing—running—at the first hurdle?

'I—I couldn't have not come,' she said, and miraculously felt the warmth she had been seeking creeping into her voice, warming the whole of her. And her courage was never higher as she said, though it had to be admitted only just loud enough for him to hear:

'I love you, Lazar.'

The words left her without her wishing them back. That was until she saw a flush of dull colour come up under his skin, watched as he closed his eyes and saw him swallow on the embarrassment she had served him. And then she too changed colour, went red, a fiery red.

Tears were in her eyes, tears of mortification that she had so misread the situation. 'I'm sorry,' she whispered, 'I've embarrassed you. I—I never meant to do that. I'll go,' she mumbled, turning, not having the least idea where she would go, but unable to bear the consequences of what she had done.

'*No!*' The word ripped from him on a hoarse sound. It had her halting, turning around. 'Do not go, Clare,' he said, his tones more even, though she could see he was nowhere near to being the controlled Lazar Vardakas she remembered as his hand lifted to rub along the back of his neck. 'Take off your coat—sit down,' he added abstractedly, in direct opposition to her stated intention to leave.

Confused, lost now to why she should stay after having embarrassed him so, she felt her moment of strength to walk away from him leave her. Perhaps he would forget she had told him she loved him, perhaps —if God was kind—Lazar would allow her to stay just these few Christmas days—she wouldn't ask for more, just to spend a few days with him.

Knowing she could deny him nothing, slowly she unbuttoned her coat and draped it over a chair. She straightened to see Lazar's eyes going over her fitted dress. At one time such a look would have had her shrinking, folding her arms in front of her, attempting to cover herself. But she didn't flinch away from his gaze and when his eyes returned to her face, she looked back bravely until he indicated that she should be seated in the chair near her. She sat down, observing that he had taken a chair some way away.

She saw as they sat facing each other that Lazar had gathered his control, looked more like the Lazar she remembered, and that in itself helped her find some self-control of her own. That was until he said gravely:

'I know it has taken you a lot of courage to come here, Clare, a lot of courage to speak of your feelings for me. You have guessed, of course, that I am heart and soul in love with you ...'

A strangled cry left her, making him break off what he was about to add, as she made to rise to her feet to go to him.

'No!' he said sharply, forcing her to stifle her impulsive action. 'Wait to hear what I have to say.'

What else was there to say? she wondered, her heart palpitating madly as she fought against tears of ecstatic joy. Lazar loved her! Lazar loved her! Her heart racing, she was compelled by the sheer authority of him to stay where she was. Soon she would be in his arms, but first it seemed he felt it necessary to say other things to her.

He waited only to see that she was comfortably settled back in her chair. 'I have told you of my love for you,' he began, his eyes drinking in her face. 'Indeed, I have been half off my head with love for you,' he confessed, to her growing wonder. 'I need you so much, Clare.'

He broke off as if trying to choose the right words, words that would not alarm her.

'Forgive my plain speaking,' he said at last, 'but my need for you, my sweet little one, has a physical side to it that I find difficult to control.' She wanted to cry out to him that she needed him in the same way, but shyness kept her silent. 'You, I know,' he said, his face stern now, 'are terrified of physical love. So how can I marry you when I know myself equally terrified that I shall not be able to keep that physical love out of our marriage?'

'Oh, Lazar,' Clare breathed softly, her eyes shining with tears as she fought against shyness to tell him how it was with her.

'I hoped for so much when I read your card,' he told her, not waiting for her to say more, and looking saddened to see the tears in her eyes. 'I just had to see you. I wanted to see you so much I made myself forget the suicidal feelings I experienced when you rejected me at the airport that last time I held you in my arms.'

'I didn't reject you.' The words came rocketing to the surface, her shyness forgotten at the hurt she received on knowing his pain. She saw his doubting look and rushed to explain. 'I was startled, that was all, shocked at the emotion in your voice. You spoke in Greek, so I had no idea what you'd said, and before I could ask, you'd gone. I only found out the week before I sent the card.'

Lazar shook his head, still doubting. 'Did I speak in Greek too that day on the beach when I had your lovely body in my arms? That day when, thrilled to have you there, I forgot myself? You ran away from me then, terrified at what I had done.'

'No, Lazar, no,' she argued. 'It may have looked like that, but I was in shock . . .'

He looked defeated suddenly as he cut in, not allowing her to finish, 'It shocked you deeply to have my touch intrude on you.'

'Yes,' she admitted truthfully. Then as she saw the way in which his hands clenched on the arms of his chair, the way he turned his head so she would not see the tormented emotion that crossed his face, she hurried on quickly, 'But only because you'd awoken something in me I didn't know was there, something in me that shocked me into realising ...'

He turned his head back to look at her, his attention all hers as his night-black eyes bored into her, causing shyness to swamp her. She fought a silent battle with shyness—and won, though she had to swallow hard before she brought out:

'You made me realise I—I didn't want you to—to stop there.'

His expression was one of disbelief, his forehead rising upwards. Silently he studied her, watching the pink colour flush over her cheeks, and sat waiting tensely as though wanting to believe her, but too afraid to dare.

'I realised when I got to my room,' Clare said, 'that— Oh God, this must sound so awfully forward. But oh, Lazar, dearest Lazar, I realised I wasn't afraid of you. I—wanted you to make love to me. It was discovering that about myself that shook me, and made me run.'

Ten years seemed to drop away from him as an incredulous, unbelieving smile started to break. 'You are sure?' he insisted, making no attempt to come anywhere near her. 'Be sure, Clare.' His voice cracked. 'Oh, my darling, be sure. I have so ached for you these long weary months. I don't think I shall be responsible for what happens once I take you in my arms—you have bolted from me before, remember.'

'I'm shy of you, Lazar,' Clare admitted, her smile beaming its way to him. 'But that's all it is.'

Slowly he rose from his chair, tall, handsome, and so heart-stoppingly the only man for her. He came forward and without volition she too was standing when he came to stop no more than a foot away from her.

'Your new style of dress suits you,' he said his voice husky. 'In itself it is an indication that I should believe you—you would not have dreamt of wearing a dress that so hinted at your womanhood last August.'

Clare stood, not moving, watching as a light kindled in his eyes as they travelled over her and rested on the contours of her breasts. And then as though he could wait no longer to have her in his arms, he moved that small step closer and very gently pulled her to him.

A sigh of pure bliss escaped Clare as she leaned her head up against the hard wall of his chest. She could feel him trembling as he held her loosely to him, held her as though afraid if he held her more tightly she might panic. He made no attempt to kiss her, but she didn't care. After all the agony of those days and nights apart from him, it was heaven just to have his arms around her, to know she hadn't got it all so wrong and that Lazar did love her—and more than that, wanted to marry her.

Lazar pulled back, gazing deeply into her eyes, his look adoring as he proceeded to examine her every feature as if he found it incredible that she should be there with him. And yet he still made no attempt to kiss her. Her eyes smiled back at him as she in turn devoured his face. Then slowly it began to dawn on her that he still wasn't a hundred per cent certain that he dare let himself go. He's *afraid* to kiss me! she thought incredulously.

Her right hand left its comfortable position at his waist. Slowly with a whispering touch her fingers came up to explore his mouth. Then gently she placed the tips of her fingers between his warm lips to part them. Shyly she raised her eyes to his.

'I've been told,' she said huskily, 'on the best authority, that you have to hold your mouth just like that when you—er—kiss.'

A deep-throated roar came from the man holding her, the most joyous sound between a laugh and the end of frustration she had ever heard. Then there was no need for her further instruction, for Lazar took over and his mouth was on her own, and he was kissing her and discovering she was eager to learn whatever else he chose to teach her.

At last he pulled back, his look burning into her eyes. She could hear his heart thudding, her own echoing the sound. 'Clare, oh, Clare!' he breathed, holding her close, seeming incapable of saying anything else in that wondrous moment but her name.

Tenderly he lifted her in his arms, carrying her to the couch and lying down beside her, his hands stroking her hair, the sides of her face. 'Clare, my Clare,' he whispered, his mouth coming down to claim hers again, setting up such a tumult of emotion inside her she just had to cling on, never wanting him to stop.

Again he pulled back and they looked deep into each other's eyes, her hand this time straying to stroke the side of his face. 'Do you know how badly I want you?' he asked, his voice quietly husky, his hands stroking possessively over her shoulder.

'I think so,' she murmured, keeping her gaze fixed on his eyes when shyness would have had her dropping her look. 'I—I feel the same way too,' she confessed. 'I think my heart will burst with it.'

His eyes were still holding hers when he placed a hand beneath her breast and felt for himself the rapid thundering of her heart.

'Hold me,' she whispered, wanting to feel the touch of his hand on her breast, but a conviction growing that he was still afraid of alarming her.

'You are not afraid?' he asked, and she knew he was aware of what she was asking.

Because it was true, she answered, 'I'm afraid of nothing with you, my darling.'

'Oh, Clare!' was wrenched from him, and then there was no holding back.

With an ecstasy of delight she felt his hand move from her heart to come gently to cup her breast, and as a shuddering sigh of pure bliss left her, she knew as he heard it and kissed her that at last he believed she feared nothing with him.

All restraint gone, she pressed to get nearer when his hand caressed to her lower spine, that hand pressing her even closer up against him, a groan escaping him at the contact of her with his hard body.

'My darling,' he murmured, one hand holding her to him and the other going to the top button of her dress, 'let me touch your soft skin.'

'Please!' Clare breathed, and so much wanted the same as him, her hands went to the buttons of his black shirt.

She stilled when she felt the delicious tingle of his hands on the satiny skin of her shoulders. Lazar stilled too, bringing back his head so he could see her face, as though suspecting that this was the moment when she would freeze on him.

'Oh, Lazar,' she breathed, her face flushed, her only

fear that he would stop making love to her, 'I wish I was lying naked next to you.'

His delight and relief were wonderful to see. 'The way we are going, my darling,' he said, a gentle teasing entering his lovemaking, 'you may get your wish.'

Clare's pink colour deepened, though how her emotions had the grace to send a deeper blush after she had made such a statement, she couldn't have said. Though Lazar seemed in no hurry as gently he slipped her bra straps aside to give him access to the love-swollen globes of her breasts. Her fingers searched inside his shirt, her hands gripping him in exquisite fervour when his mouth lightly secured the tip of her breast.

'Oh, Lazar,' came from her in a frenzied whisper of desire. 'Oh, my darling, I want you—I want you!'

A rejoicing look was on him as his caressing hand took over her breast from his lips, and his mouth claimed hers. 'There is no hurry, my darling,' he told her tenderly. 'I want it to be so right for you. Just ride with it for a while.' He smiled down into her face, all the love in the world there for her in his look. Then, his hands leaving her body, he cupped her face in his hands. 'My sweet Clare,' he said huskily, 'I love you.' He placed a gentle kiss on her mouth. Then while she just looked at him, her heart full, they both heard the sound of car doors thudding closed.

'*Theos, ohi!*' rang from him, and she knew then from that heartfelt '*God, no!*' that Lazar was nowhere near as cool as he would have her believe in breaking through any barriers there might be in his initiation of her. He must then have remembered something their lovemaking had driven from his mind, for he muttered, 'I had forgotten,' and then he was sitting up, helping her to sit up too.

He helped her to straighten her clothing before he attended to his own, making sure she was neatly buttoned up before fastening the buttons on his shirt.

His expression was half angry, half rueful when he looked at her, both of them now sitting decorously on the couch, for all he kept his arm around her.

'I think I have in my way been as frightened as you, my Clare,' he told her softly. 'I was too scared to meet you at the airport in case I said the wrong thing and got off to a bad start—I was not sure if that happened that it would not affect my driving and have us both injured in a car smash . . .'

'So that's why Rasmus met me,' she said, only now beginning to realise the effect she had on him.

He nodded. 'I had no idea what would happen either when Rasmus did get you here,' he said, talking quickly now, wanting this explanation out of the way before his callers were shown in. 'I knew my self-control was a puny vessel where you are concerned— I had not meant to come to say goodbye to you when you went away from me. I left it too late, or so I thought, then I found myself in my car racing to Micra because I just had to see you once more. And so after speaking to you this morning—what a joy it was to hear your voice!'—he broke off to give her a smile that warmed her through and through, 'I rang my parents telling them to drop everything, that it was imperative that they got here by tonight.'

Bereft of words, trying desperately to come back to earth after the thrilling explosion of his lovemaking, Clare grasped at what he was saying. He had felt himself so out of control where she was concerned he had sent for his parents, knowing she would be safe from him while they were in residence at the villa.

'Oh, Lazar,' was all she could manage, on a choky little whisper.

'Oh, Clare,' he teased in an effort to bring her temperature down. Then with his other hand holding her two in a firm grip, he said, 'Perhaps it will work well that they have arrived.'

'Work well?' she queried, trying to put her intelligence to use, but having no idea what he was meaning.

'You and I will go to England tomorrow for me to speak with your father. If it would please you I will ask my parents to come with us so we can have a family celebration.'

'You're going to see my father tomorrow?' she gasped, her mind only capable of dealing with one part of what he had said as she wondered if she would ever get used to the way Lazar used aeroplanes as casually as she and her mother used the Mini.

'Of course,' he said, a proud look coming to him. 'Tomorrow is the twenty-fifth—it doesn't leave much time to make the arrangements.'

'Arrangements?'

Lazar gave her an adoring look. 'I insist you must be my wife before this year is out, my Clare.'

Clare was still trying to get her breath back when footsteps were heard coming along the hall.

'My beloved little one,' Lazar said huskily, observing she looked a shade nervous to be about to meet his parents, 'they are going to love their new daughter.' He smiled, a smile that told her she was the keeper of his heart. 'Who could help but love you?' he said tenderly. Their lips met in a gentle touch—a door opened.

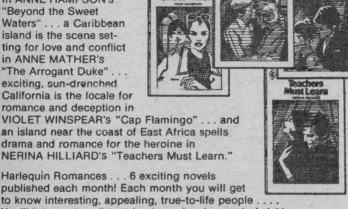